The SWEETEST CHRISTMAS

MICHELLE WILLINGHAM

The characters and events portrayed in this book are fictitious. Any similarity to persons, living or dead, is coincidental and not intended by the author.

Text copyright © 2017 Michelle Willingham
Excerpt from *A Dance with the Devil* © 2016
by Michelle Willingham.

ALL RIGHTS RESERVED

No part of this book may be reproduced, or stored in a retrieval system, or transmitted in any form or by any means electronic, mechanical, photocopying, recording, or otherwise, without express written permission of the author.

Published by Michelle Willingham
www.michellewillingham.com

ISBN-13: 978-0-9906345-8-4

Cover by Frauke Spanuth/Croco Designs
Photo by Period Images
Interior formatting by Author E.M.S.

Published in the United States of America.

OTHER BOOKS BY MICHELLE WILLINGHAM

Untamed Highlanders
(Regency)
The Highlander and the Governess

A Most Peculiar Season Series
(Regency)
A Viking for the Viscountess
A Viking Maiden for the Marquess

Secrets in Silk Series
(Regency Scotland)
Undone by the Duke
Unraveled by the Rebel
Undressed by the Earl
Unlaced by the Outlaw

The Earls Next Door Series
(Victorian England)
Good Earls Don't Lie
What the Earl Needs Now

Forbidden Viking Series
(Viking Age Ireland)
To Sin with a Viking
To Tempt a Viking

Warriors of Ireland Series
(Medieval Ireland)
Warrior of Ice
Warrior of Fire

MacEgan Brothers Series
(Medieval Ireland)
Her Warrior Slave
"The Viking's Forbidden Love-Slave" (novella)
Her Warrior King
Her Irish Warrior
The Warrior's Touch
Taming Her Irish Warrior
"The Warrior's Forbidden Virgin" (novella)
"Voyage of an Irish Warrior" (novella)
Surrender to an Irish Warrior
"Pleasured by the Viking" (novella)
"Lionheart's Bride" (novella)
Warriors in Winter

The MacKinloch Clan Series
(Medieval Scotland)
Claimed by the Highland Warrior
Seduced by Her Highland Warrior
"Craving the Highlander's Touch" (novella)
Tempted by the Highland Warrior
"Rescued by the Highland Warrior" (novella in the *Highlanders* anthology)

The Accidental Series
(Victorian England/Fictional Province of Lohenberg)
"An Accidental Seduction" (novella)
The Accidental Countess
The Accidental Princess
The Accidental Prince

Other Titles
"Innocent in the Harem"
(A novella of the sixteenth-century Ottoman Empire)

"A Wish to Build a Dream On"
(time travel novella to medieval Ireland)

The Castle Keyvnor Series
"A Dance with the Devil"
(Regency Halloween novella)

"The Sweetest Christmas"
(Regency Christmas novella)

Chapter One

To Lady Marjorie Hambly, the idea of marriage was like being poked in the eye with a sharp stick.

Unlike her four sisters, she had no interest in finding a husband. At least, not after the last nightmare of a suitor had ruined her girlish dreams.

Her life had been overrun with decorations, gowns, flowers, and guests arriving for the weddings of her sisters, Tamsyn and Morgan, this Christmas. It *should* have been terribly exciting—except that she felt rather lonely at the thought of her family dividing up and moving away. Even her younger sisters, Rose and Gwyn, had decided to seek husbands among the guests.

But not Marjorie.

Oh, she knew the sort of noblemen her mother had invited to the wedding. Dukes, earls, barons, and knights—anyone her father deemed appropriate as a guest, and particularly those whom he wanted to match up with his daughters. But Marjorie was determined not to fall into that trap again. She would celebrate at the wedding, dance, and make merry, until every last gentleman was gone. Then, and only then, would she breathe a sigh of relief.

Was it unkind to hope that Rose and Gwyn wouldn't find a suitor among the guests? They were both so young, and Marjorie didn't want her life to change, living alone with her parents. More than anything, she needed to find a distraction—something to occupy her time and to divert her attention from the impending weddings. Or worse, the not-so-subtle insinuations from elderly matrons that she was somehow lacking, since her own engagement had ended a month ago.

But she didn't care. She was well rid of Robert Hanford, Viscount Dewbury, and thankfully, she had made her parents see what a controlling tyrant he was. Lord Dewbury had wanted an obedient dog, not a wife, and she was deeply grateful that his days of ruling her life were over.

"Cousin Marjorie," came a soft voice from behind her. She turned and saw Ariadne Cushing approaching while her parents gave orders to the servants collecting their trunks and valises. The young woman wore spectacles and her gown and gloves were smudged with ink. Her blond hair was bundled tightly beneath her bonnet, and she gave a tentative smile.

Marjorie smiled and embraced her cousin. "I am glad you could come to Castle Keyvnor for the weddings, Ariadne."

Her cousin's expression was hesitant. "I am happy for your sisters, and of course, we look forward to sharing Christmas with you and your family."

"You don't…look particularly happy," Marjorie ventured. "Is something wrong?"

"No." Then she amended, "Well, yes. Sort of. What I mean is that…I need your help." She linked her arm in Marjorie's, and the pair of them walked down the hallway.

She didn't know her cousin all that well, so it struck her as odd that Ariadne would reach out for assistance. "What do you need?"

Her cousin's face was bright red, and she admitted, "I need a husband. Before we leave this castle." Her lips tightened into a line, and she looked all the world as if she wanted to fall through the floor.

A husband is the last thing you need, Marjorie thought to herself, shuddering at the idea. But then, she took a closer look at her cousin's pained face and wondered if some scandal had befallen her. "Why so soon?"

"Mother has told me that she will choose my husband for me after Christmas," Ariadne answered. "She says that I haven't the common sense of a flea and that I should give the matter over into her hands."

Marjorie wasn't entirely surprised. Aunt Agnes was quite abrasive in her manners and she had no qualms about stepping on Ariadne's feelings. But then, she realized that there *was* an opportunity here. Her mother had invited many eligible bachelors for the sake of her sisters. And if Ariadne wanted one of them, what harm was there? She should put her personal feelings aside, for not every man was like Lord Dewbury.

"So…you want me to introduce you to gentlemen, and you'll choose one yourself?"

"Exactly," Ariadne said. Worry creased her forehead again. "But no man would ever talk to me." She grimaced and tugged at her gloves. "I know I'm not a beauty. And, well, I'm a bit of a bluestocking. That's why I need your help."

Marjorie led her cousin up the stairs toward the room she would share with her sister. "What do you want me to do?"

"I will pick out the gentleman, and I need you to talk to him for me."

Marjorie had the sudden vision of saying to a stranger, *Pardon me, but my cousin would like to marry you.* No, that wouldn't do at all. "Ariadne, you really should speak to him yourself."

"Oh, I will. Eventually. But I would like you to help me pick a man out, and then I will decide if he's suitable for me. Someone quiet and not too handsome."

Her cousin made it sound as if choosing a husband was like buying a new hat. Marjorie paused before Ariadne's door and said, "Don't set your sights too low, Cousin. You might find someone wonderful when you least expect it."

Truthfully, the gentlemen her father had invited were among the most sought-after bachelors of the ton. She couldn't recall if any of them were homely or dull. At the same time, Marjorie did understand her cousin's desire to find a man who was not at the center of attention.

She excused herself to let Ariadne get settled in her room and decided to see which gentlemen had arrived for the wedding. It was likely that they would be in the billiards room, and she could examine the choices from the hallway.

It was best to find a man who was meek and manageable, someone who might have trouble finding a bride. It would give Ariadne confidence in speaking with him.

As she walked down the hallway, Marjorie heard the faint sounds of lute music, and the hair stood up on the back of her neck. "Not today," she muttered. An icy chill gusted over her, and she shivered, hurrying down the stairs.

She knew of at least three ghosts who haunted Castle Keyvnor, but there were likely more. She was well-acquainted with a Tudor ghost named Benedict, as well as the ghost of the late Lady Banfield's drowned five-year-old son, Paul. And then, there was the pirate ghost, whom they had nicknamed the Man in Black. Marjorie shuddered at the memory. *He* was the most vicious of all.

The castle ghosts delighted in teasing her. She would walk into a room and suddenly, a frigid blast of air would surround her shoulders. Sometimes, Marjorie heard them singing or talking, which was even worse. She didn't know if anyone else heard them, but it made her question what was real and what was not.

It was yet another reason she didn't want her sisters to be married—for then, the ghosts could devote all their attention toward tormenting her.

Marjorie hurried down the stairs, bolting toward the billiards room. The frozen shadows seemed to follow her, and she distinctively heard the sound of mocking laughter behind her. She turned her head and glared at the empty hallway, letting the ghosts know she did *not* appreciate their tricks.

She slowed her pace when she reached the doorway of the billiards room. She didn't want any of the men to see her, but she could steal a peek from the doorway.

There was no question of the sort of man she was looking for. Someone not engaged in conversation, possibly lurking in the shadows. Perhaps one who was shy and not very attractive. She pressed her hands to the doorway, peering inside.

Lord Blackwater was playing billiards with Lord Snowingham, better known as Snow. No, neither one would do. They were both rakishly handsome. Four other gentlemen were playing cards at another table, but Marjorie dismissed them all. They were all too wealthy and bold—two traits that often transformed into arrogance.

She overheard Lord Michael Beck thanking Snow and Blackwater for their hospitality and letting him stay in their room. It didn't surprise her that he'd have to share, since every room in the castle was occupied by wedding guests.

Marjorie continued to inspect the men, and a smile curved over her face as she saw the tall, dark-haired man standing in the corner. He seemed to be watching the others, and there was a quiet sense of solitude surrounding him. If she hadn't been looking for such a man, she might not have noticed him at all.

Perfect.

At first glance, he *did* seem rather ordinary. His dark brown hair was neatly groomed, and he wore a black coat, a black waistcoat, and tan breeches. Nothing that would attract any attention whatsoever.

But when his gaze shifted to the doorway, his expression faltered—almost as if he had seen her.

Marjorie didn't move, for she might have imagined it. Yet, she sensed his stare, and a strange ripple of awareness crossed over her. Would he suit Ariadne at all? She decided to find out who he was, and speak with him at the first opportunity.

The sound of a throat clearing behind her interrupted her musings. Marjorie turned and saw Mrs. Bray, the housekeeper. The older woman's dark hair was scraped beneath a cap, and her apron stretched across her portly frame.

"Lady Marjorie, your mother would not approve of this," the housekeeper began.

"Approve of my walking down the hallway?" Marjorie answered breezily. "I hardly think that's a sin."

Before the housekeeper could chide her again, she retreated from the entrance to the billiards room, behaving as if she'd done nothing wrong. Which she hadn't, truly. She lived here, and if she wanted to peruse the billiards room, there was no harm in it.

A sense of satisfaction filled her at the thought of the man in the corner of the room. He might do very well for Ariadne, particularly if he was shy.

She rather hoped he was.

֍

Sir William Crandall took a slow, steady breath. Though he'd known that Castle Keyvnor would be immensely crowded with arriving wedding guests, he had hoped he could keep a firm command upon his senses. Whenever he was in the midst of a large group, his pulse quickened and his lungs seemed to tighten. It was maddening the way he had no control over the suffocating feelings.

Despite his discomfort among crowds, he'd promised his sister that he would come to the wedding. She had claimed that he needed to escape the oppressive prison of the house. But there was another reason why he had come—to face his past mistakes and move on with his life.

The need to escape and take a breath of fresh air was undeniable, so William made his excuses and walked into the hallway. Earlier, he had noticed a young lady spying at the doorway, and he half-wondered if she was still lingering in the hall. As he passed through the door, he caught the faint scent of lavender.

William walked toward the opposite end of the hall, for beyond the second corridor, he'd spied a door that led outside to the garden. The idea of a peaceful retreat was exactly what he needed now. He wanted to be alone without anyone to bother him.

There was an unusual chill in the air, and he hastened his steps to escape the draft. Just as he was about to round the corner, he heard a strange laugh. It held a wicked tone, as if someone were mocking him.

William continued around the corner but collided into the young woman, who had been walking the opposite way. "I beg your pardon," he said, feeling foolish that he'd knocked her to the floor. He held out a gloved hand. "I didn't see you."

She took his hand and stood, straightening her skirts. A few strawberry blond curls had escaped her updo, and she tucked them back into place. "It's all right. I had hoped to have a word with you, and I suppose this will do well enough."

William wasn't certain what to make of that. Why would she want to speak with him? He had never seen her until today. "I'm sorry, but I don't think we've met before."

"You are right, of course. But I saw you just a few moments ago, and I think you might be perfect for her."

Her? William hadn't the faintest notion what the woman was talking about. But he had a feeling he wouldn't like what she had to say. "If you'll excuse me, I meant to go outside to take some air."

"An excellent idea," she agreed. "I shall come with you."

He stared down at her, for he didn't want company. Then he found an appropriate excuse to dissuade her. "We haven't a chaperone." With a nod, he added, "Another time, perhaps."

She shrugged. "Our conversation won't be longer than two minutes, I promise you." Then she took his arm and guided him around the corner. "Now, then, let's begin with names. I am Lady Marjorie Hambly, and my father is Lord Banfield. My sisters are getting married, and I presume you are one of the wedding guests."

He nodded again. "I am Sir William Crandall."

"Sir William," she said quietly, as if testing out his name. "Yes, I think that will do nicely. It's a very common name, not bold or demanding at all."

Against his better judgment, he asked, "Are you criticizing my name?"

"No, not at all. William is a very traditional name, and I do believe it will be perfect."

For what? His brows furrowed, and he decided that the woman was daft. Right now, he wanted nothing more than to leave in peace. "Good day, Lady Marjorie." With that, he strode away, toward the doors leading outside.

"No, wait! You can't leave yet. Not until I've told you about the bargain."

William ignored her and continued walking, though he heard her hurrying after him. He'd had quite enough of this nonsensical conversation. Right now, all he wanted was to sit in peaceful silence, perhaps by a fountain or a tree, with no one around.

But Lady Marjorie flung herself in front of the door. "Two minutes of your time, Sir William. That's all I need."

Her face was flushed, and he found himself staring at her mouth. She had intriguing lips, with the lower lip fuller than the top. He hadn't any notion what it was she wanted, but he guessed he would have no peace and quiet until he let her have her say.

He pulled out his pocket watch, glanced at the time, and then motioned for her to go on. "Only two. You may begin."

She blinked at that, but then said, "You are unmarried, and I can only guess that you are a very shy gentleman."

He wasn't at all shy. He simply didn't like people. But her assessment was so earnest, he couldn't help but ask, "Why would you believe I am shy?"

"Well, you must be. You were standing in the corner, speaking with no one, after all."

"I like corners." And he liked being alone even more.

"Perhaps. But if you intend to find a wife, it's not the best place to find one."

Personally, William thought a darkened corner was an excellent place to get acquainted with a woman. Particularly if they were alone in the shadows, and if her lower lip was slightly larger than the top. He would take command of that mouth, kissing her until she grew breathless.

But then, he had no intention of getting married anymore, so it hardly mattered.

"My cousin, Ariadne Cushing, is in need of a husband, and she wants a gentleman who is quiet and shy, like yourself. She asked me to help her find someone, and I said I should be glad to assist. Would you like to meet her?"

Now it was beginning to make sense. Lady Marjorie considered herself a matchmaker and had selected him as her next victim. "Why would you think I have any interest in being married?"

"Because every man needs an heir."

"Not I. I have three older brothers with sons of their own and a sister. I could happily remain a bachelor for the rest of my life," he pointed out.

"Oh." Lady Marjorie bit her lower lip, as if she hadn't considered this. It drew his attention back to her mouth, and his thoughts took a wayward stroll toward kissing again.

William put away his pocket watch and said, "Your time is up, Lady Marjorie." He put his hands on either side of her, intending to open the door leading outside to the garden. But the knob wouldn't budge. He turned it both directions and then shrugged. "It's locked."

"No, it isn't." Marjorie never moved from her place, her brown eyes staring back at him. "It doesn't have a lock." She reached behind her for the knob, and her gloved hand brushed against his. The light touch sent a flare of heat within him. He grew very aware of the scent of her skin, like crushed lavender.

"Will you at least think about meeting her?" she murmured. "You might like Ariadne very much, once you get to know her."

He took her hand and brought it back in front of him. Her eyes widened as he held it a moment. Then he peeled back the edge of her glove and drew her inner wrist to his mouth. He wanted to unnerve her, to send a blatant message.

He kissed her pulse, and heard her shaky intake of breath.

"Don't meddle with other people's lives, Lady Marjorie. And stay out of mine."

༄

Men could be infuriating sometimes. The more she thought of it, the more Marjorie was convinced that William and Ariadne could make an outstanding match with one another. Both were quiet and did not like crowds of people. Sir William struck her as a very intelligent man, despite his tendency to lurk. And he was handsome in his own way. Not in the jaw-dropping—dearest Mama *please* introduce me to that magnificent specimen—sort of way, but he did have nice eyes. They were blue with a dark rim of gray around them. And though he was taller than most men, she didn't think he was gangly or weak.

Quite the contrary. His build had a lean tautness, which she'd noticed when she'd stumbled into him.

But Sir William was stubborn and didn't seem to want a wife. It was clear that he wouldn't even give Ariadne a chance, although she completely understood his reluctance to marry. Earlier, during supper, he had chosen a seat far away from everyone and had not spoken a word.

Marjorie was determined to find a way to pair them up. If Ariadne didn't like him, so be it. But she intended to do her best to bring them together tonight.

She crossed through the Great Hall, where the servants were busy hanging garlands of fir and sprigs of holly. An enormous Yule log would be lit in two days, for the Christmas Eve weddings. And her sister Gwyn had suggested that mistletoe be hung in discreet corners.

It made her think of Sir William once again. He had unraveled her senses when he'd kissed the bare skin of her wrist, making her wonder why he'd done it. Was he trying to intimidate her? Instead, it had evoked the opposite effect—her skin had flushed with awareness and a sudden interest that she'd tried to tamp down.

Clearly, her brain had forgotten that even handsome men could be troublesome. She was starting to realize that Sir William was not quite as pliable as she'd believed. Nonetheless, tonight she planned to introduce him to Ariadne. Hopefully, he might give the young woman a chance. If he preferred quiet, shy women, then they would be an excellent match for one another. Though he'd said he had no intention of marrying, she wanted to believe it was because he hadn't met the right woman yet.

And perhaps, if she made two people happy, it would take her mind off her own failures.

"Marjorie!" she heard a voice call out from behind her. It was Jane, her dearest friend, along with her new husband, Devon Lancaster.

Marjorie embraced Jane and beamed at the sight of them. "It's so wonderful to see you," she gushed. "Have you only just arrived?"

"We have, yes. But I've heard that there are not many places to stay. We may need to find rooms at Hollybrook Park." Jane exchanged a glance with Devon, who was talking with another guest.

"Don't worry. As our invited guests, we have a room saved for you." Marjorie walked beside her dearest friend, nodding in greeting to Mr. Lancaster. Jane held her husband's hand, and there was a flush of love and joy upon her face. Marriage certainly agreed with Jane, and Marjorie was delighted for both of them.

"I will have Mrs. Bray set out food and drinks for you in the parlor, since we've only just finished the evening meal. You may join us in a game of cards, once you've finished," she suggested.

"I would be grateful for food," Mr. Lancaster answered. He shot a devilish smile toward his wife. "And the parlor sounds perfect."

Marjorie gave the orders, and when they departed, she saw Sir William leaving the dining room last. He was avoiding people again, it seemed. She was fairly certain that Ariadne had gone with her mother to play cards, and that was the perfect way to introduce them.

She approached Sir William and smiled brightly. "Won't you join in the games? There will be music as well. And you can meet Miss Cushing, if you like."

"I'll let everyone else enjoy the merriment," he said, beckoning for her to go. "Find someone else for Miss Cushing."

She hesitated, studying his face. The man was adamant about not even contemplating the subject or marriage. "May I ask you a question?" She kept her voice low, so no one would hear her.

"You already have."

She took a step closer to him. "Why did you come to my sisters' weddings?"

"To prove a point to someone," he admitted. "But she isn't here, so it hardly matters anymore. And I promised my sister I would attend."

Now *that* whetted her curiosity even more. It sounded very much like a thwarted love story, and she tried to remember which guests hadn't arrived.

"Don't you think you should try to have a pleasant Christmas?" Marjorie asked. "We have so many things planned so that everyone will have a reason to celebrate. Will you not attempt to find joy in the season?"

"There is no joy in the Christmas season," he said in a clipped voice. In his blue eyes, she saw the shadow of pain, and a sudden sadness washed over her at his words. How could anyone believe that? Something truly terrible must have happened to him during Christmas. Whether it was a family member or a lost love, she didn't know. But it bothered her deeply to see someone unhappy during her favorite holiday.

Sir William stepped away to the door. "Now, if you will excuse me—"

"No," Marjorie blurted out. Something had to be done. She could not stand aside and let this man suffer in silence. Though she didn't know what had happened, she felt compelled to help him. "As the daughter of your host, I will not excuse you."

He did pause at that. "What?"

She fumbled around for a reason and said, "I want you to join us in the games tonight. You might find a bit of amusement in them."

"I intend to find a book in your library," he countered. "Perhaps I'll find another corner in which I may lurk. Enjoy your games."

She joined him at the doorway, not wanting him to retreat again. He wouldn't listen to reason, but perhaps he would listen to a threat. "If you don't come, I shall tell all the mothers that you are seeking a bride. They will be falling all over themselves to offer their daughters. You'll never get a moment's peace."

He did turn back at that, his face tight with frustration. "Is this a declaration of war?"

She only smiled. "Let us call it an incentive."

"I mistakenly thought that the daughter of Lord Banfield would be a more considerate hostess. Why would you make such a demand?"

She gripped her gloved hands together. "Because it will not kill you to smile at a young woman and meet her. Enjoy a night of Christmas fun, and put the past behind you."

"We should make a wager in a game of whist," he offered. "If I win, you'll leave me in peace and tell all the matrons that I intend to remain a bachelor."

She did smile at that, for she was quite good at cards. And cheating, if the need called for it, which this certainly did. "Very well. But if I win, you will be kind to my cousin Ariadne. You will converse and perhaps even dance with her at the Yule ball after the wedding."

"I don't dance," he shot back. "And you should prepare to lose, Lady Marjorie."

She laughed at that. "I never lose."

Chapter Two

The parlor was freezing cold. No matter how he adjusted his seat, William could not rid himself of the chill.

He had reluctantly agreed to partner in whist with Miss Ariadne Cushing, but they could hardly win a trick at all. It was almost as if Lady Marjorie knew which cards they were holding, though he had no idea how it was possible for her to cheat. Sometimes she glanced at the air behind him, as if she saw something, but there was nothing there at all. Her partner was the elderly Lady Octavia, the dowager Viscountess of North Barrows, who appeared gleeful at their winning streak.

William got his own petty revenge through silence. He knew Lady Marjorie wanted to match him up with Miss Cushing, but he would not be manipulated by her wiles. Instead, he simply played one hand after another, trying to win. His partner clutched her cards, and her face blushed a furious red.

"I say, I *am* enjoying this game," Lady Octavia proclaimed. She laid down her trump card and pulled the stack toward her. "It's a pity I didn't place a bet on it."

"But I did," Marjorie beamed. After William laid down his next card, she trumped him and smiled. "I do hope Sir William does not hold it against me." Then she tried to engage him in conversation again. "Do tell us about your home in Warfield. I should love to hear about it."

He pretended as if she hadn't spoken. Lady Octavia appeared oblivious, and he suspected she had difficulty hearing. Miss Cushing seemed bewildered by all of it. She adjusted her spectacles and feigned an interest in her cards.

From beside him, Lady Marjorie nudged him with her knee. Her purpose was obvious: *Answer the question.*

William nudged his own knee against hers. *No.*

At that, she glared at him. *Stop being difficult.*

He had no intention of it. She was the one being difficult, trying to matchmake him with a woman when he didn't want to be matchmade. Or matched. Whatever the right word was.

But it would be rude not to answer, so he nodded to Lady Octavia. "It's near Wales."

"Wales is such a beautiful country," Marjorie remarked. "So wild and untamed, don't you think?"

He shrugged. "I haven't been there since last spring. I've left it in the care of my sister and older brothers."

"Isn't that a coincidence?" Marjorie beamed. "Miss Cushing has brothers, too! You have a great deal in common."

Good God, the woman truly was reaching for anything to pair them up. He almost felt sorry for Miss Cushing. The woman appeared terrified of him, but he wasn't about to give Lady Marjorie the satisfaction of a conversation.

"I'm so sorry," Miss Cushing whispered. "But I cannot trump her." She turned over her last card, looking humiliated at the loss.

In the meantime, Marjorie pulled the pile of cards toward her. "And since that's the last trick, I believe Lady Octavia and I have won the game. Sir William, why don't you walk with Miss Cushing and show her the refreshments over there? Mother has arranged some delicious tarts and desserts."

He was tempted to call her bluff by declining, but the glint in her eye nearly dared him to try it. With a sigh, he stood from the table. As he walked past her, he murmured, "I know you cheated. And I'm going to find out how."

Marjorie only smiled.

༃

Once he had gone, Marjorie glanced at his empty chair. Above him was Benedict, the Tudor ghost. He was beaming at her, and she nodded her head in thanks. Benedict was one of the friendlier specters, and they had a standing arrangement. As long as she allowed him to play his lute for an hour, while she listened as his audience, he helped her at cards.

And Marjorie wasn't above cheating when the outcome was meant to help a family member. She sat back in her chair, watching Sir William and Miss Cushing. They stood at the refreshment table with glasses of lemonade, neither looking at each other nor speaking.

"Awkward, aren't they?" Lady Octavia said. "I don't know why you thought to match them up."

"Both of them are shy and quiet," Marjorie explained. "I thought I'd simply help Cousin Ariadne find someone suitable."

"You're trying to match up a dragon with a mouse, that's what."

"Sir William is *not* a dragon," Marjorie argued.

"Who said I was speaking of Sir William?" the old woman cackled. Then she rapped her cane on the floor and leaned in. "But of course, he is a fine figure of a man. A bit handsome and brooding."

"He doesn't like people."

"*I* don't like people, either," Lady Octavia pronounced. "But if you ask me, I think you're sending the wrong girl after him."

Marjorie was beginning to wonder that herself. Sir William had obliged her, but he looked uncomfortable beside Miss Cushing. The young woman was staring at her untouched plate of cake, her lips unmoving. It appeared to be rather disastrous.

"Then what sort of gentleman should I match up with Ariadne?" She asked the question aloud without thinking. It wasn't as if Octavia would know the answer.

"I don't know about your cousin, but I *know* what was happening beneath the table, Lady Marjorie." The old woman's gaze narrowed. "My knees were bumped and jostled several times."

"I'm sorry." In spite of herself, Marjorie felt her cheeks flush. "I was frustrated with him for not speaking during the game."

"He was baiting you. And I rather think you enjoyed it." Lady Octavia leaned against her cane and stood. "Now, I'm off to get some sleep. Perhaps you should borrow Miss Cushing's spectacles. You seem to be quite blind about what's really going on." With a knowing smile, the woman hobbled away.

Marjorie wanted to groan. Was that how it had seemed to everyone else? She hadn't intended any sort of interaction with Sir William.

"All right. I'll go and rescue them." She pushed back her chair and walked toward the table. Her cousin stood apart from William, picking at her slice of cake.

"Is something wrong, Ariadne?" Marjorie asked. "Do you not like the cake?"

Her cousin risked a glance back at her, and her face held only misery. "The cake is fine," she whispered.

Marjorie patted her cousin's shoulder and then walked to the opposite end of the table where Sir William was standing. She dropped her voice low. "What did you say to her? She looks as if you just killed her pet kitten."

Sir William shrugged and dug his fork into his own slice of cake. "I assure you, I did no such thing."

"You're not even trying," she sighed. "I thought the two of you might have a great deal in common."

"We both have brothers, as you noted." He took another bite of cake, and a crumb clung to his mouth. Marjorie nearly pointed it out to him, but her attention was captivated by that firm mouth. His blue eyes stared back at her with amusement, and she had a sudden vision of kissing him and licking the crumb away.

Good heavens. What was wrong with her?

"I *did* speak to her," he added. "I asked her about her family and whether she was looking forward to the wedding. She never said a word."

Marjorie was about to beckon her cousin to come closer, but Ariadne had fled to her mother's side. "Apparently, I am a terrible matchmaker."

"Why would you want to meddle in people's lives?" William asked. "Leave them alone, and if they want to come together on their own, they will."

"It never happens that way." Marjorie reached for her own cake, still distracted by the firm corners of his mouth. She took a bite of the spice cake, reveling in the sweetness. "Oh my. I think I've just tasted a bit of heaven."

"It *is* good, isn't it?" he remarked. "This is my second piece."

"I'm only supposed to have a bite or two. Ladies can never indulge." But she savored the sweetness, loving the flavor.

"Lady Marjorie, it's not a good idea to—" His words broke off, and she opened her eyes.

"To what?"

He whispered, "To look at your cake as if it's a long-lost lover."

"If I could marry cake, I would." She smiled and discreetly licked her lips. "Cake would never tell me what to do or take my fortune away, leaving me with only pin money. Cake would never make unreasonable demands. Cake *understands* me."

He laughed at that. "You, Lady Marjorie, are nothing like I expected."

"And you, Sir William, have spoken more in the past two minutes than I've ever heard you say."

He set down his plate and took a sip of lemonade. "Perhaps that's because I know you have no desire to marry. And that is why I can speak freely."

"Heaven forbid I should become another man's property." With reluctance, she set down her empty plate. She was so grateful to be rid of Lord Dewbury. The man had actually tried to dictate the gowns she wore and the food she ate. She shuddered at the memory.

"And yet, you're still trying to throw your cousin upon the sacrificial altar."

"That's different. Ariadne *wants* to be married." Though her cousin wanted to have a choice in her suitor. Marjorie could only imagine the sort of man Aunt Agnes would choose for her daughter. The thought was not at all pleasant.

"I'm not certain she does," Sir William countered. "At least, not to someone like me. She could hardly speak two sentences."

"I imagine you intimidated her." She hadn't expected Sir William to be so...forthright, and likely it had put Ariadne's brain at sixes and sevens.

"I am not at all intimidating." He finished his lemonade and eyed the cake as if contemplating a third piece.

"Not to me," she acceded. "I will admit that I misjudged you. I thought you would be a shy gentleman in need of a wife."

He rolled his eyes. "I am a man who likes peace and quiet. And while Ariadne is quiet enough, she and I would never suit. Besides that, the last thing I want is a wife."

She wanted to tell him that she fully agreed with him about avoiding marriage. But that wouldn't help her cousin at all.

"Perhaps you haven't met the right lady yet," she suggested. The more she talked with Sir William, the more she wondered what sort of woman would suit him. "You could make someone a very good husband. You *are* a knight, after all."

He eyed her thoughtfully. "Many women would not even consider me because a knighthood is not a high rank."

"How did you become a knight?" she asked.

His countenance reddened as if he didn't want to speak of it. But then he admitted, "I was merely at the right place at the right time. I defended the king from a man trying to harm him."

His reluctance to discuss the matter only raised him in her esteem. He could easily have boasted about the accomplishment, but instead, he preferred to suppress his deed.

"It sounds as if you are an honorable man. I do think you could win the heart of a woman like Ariadne, if you tried."

"And I have *brothers*," he mocked.

She smiled back at him. It had been a stretch, trying to find some commonality between him and Ariadne. "Whereas I have no brothers at all."

"Thank God. There is no chance at all of a match between someone like you and me." The teasing smile at his lips made her answer with her own smile.

"Heaven forbid." She raised her glass in a silent toast. There was a nonchalant manner about him, and she found it entirely too easy to talk with William about nothing at all. "Now that we've settled that, will you help me find a better match for my cousin?"

"You want *me* to play matchmaker?" His brows narrowed at the idea.

"Well, why not? You do know many of the wedding guests. Is there someone better who would suit my cousin?"

"I don't even know her."

"You know how shy she is. Surely you could think of someone."

"I have no desire to spoil the life of a friend by ensnaring him into an unwanted marriage."

She could almost understand his point, but this was different. "I'm asking about someone who *does* want to find a wife. Cousin Ariadne has an acceptable dowry, and she's not bad-looking." When she removed her spectacles and washed the ink from her hands, that is. "Think upon it, won't you?"

Without waiting for a reply, she left him standing beside the table.

౪

William hadn't slept well at all. The castle was completely crowded with guests, and although he had been given a small room with a narrow bed, he'd been unable to calm his troubled thoughts.

He'd spent hours last night staring at the ceiling. Lady Marjorie's whiskey brown eyes had been fraught with mischief, and her strawberry blond hair framed a beautiful face. But it was her lips that captivated him. He'd daydreamed of silencing her chatter by claiming that mouth and kissing her senseless.

It had surprised him at how relaxed he'd been around Lady Marjorie. Like himself, she had no desire to marry, and he had enjoyed the challenge of resisting her match with Miss Cushing. Poor Miss Cushing had been so tongue-tied, it had been impossible to form any sort of conversation. But once Lady Marjorie had accepted that they were not suited, he'd enjoyed bantering with her.

Although, he admitted to himself, he was the very last person who would help her with matchmaking. Her request last night, that he could help find a suitor for the timid Miss Cushing, was nothing he would ever consider—just like the idea of finding another bride to marry.

He had walked that path before, a year ago, and it had ended in utter humiliation. There was nothing worse than standing beside the minister, waiting for a bride who never arrived. Or having to give explanations about why she had run away.

When he'd received this invitation to the Hambly

weddings, he'd immediately wanted to decline. But his former bride, Miss Laurie Kent, had been invited. And he wanted to face her, proving that he had moved on with his life.

Although damn it all, he hadn't.

He'd spent the last year brooding, carrying out his responsibilities, and living in his brothers' shadow. He'd already resigned himself to a life of solitude. He hoped to keep a small house with only a handful of servants and blessed silence and peace. He didn't need anyone else, nor did he want any sort of life except one confined to solitude. That would suit him just fine. He was thankful that his investments had paid handsomely, and it gave him the financial freedom to do as he pleased.

And that meant he had no need to marry.

Throughout the morning, he had tried to stay out of the way, lurking in corners. He'd seen Nathaniel Cushing dart out of the library and speak hastily with Miss Daphne Goodenham in a nearby parlor. For a moment, he'd wondered if she was all right, but then Cushing led her outside toward the gardens, and she went with him willingly. He contemplated whether to follow, but ended up running into his friend, Hal, Viscount Blackwater.

"You seem in good spirits," William remarked, stepping into the hallway.

"I am getting married, after all," Blackwater answered. A smile edged his mouth before it tightened. "But I wouldn't mind escaping the castle for an hour or two." He paused for a moment, his gaze on the floor, and murmured, "They speak of ghosts here. I suppose you've heard the rumors?"

"Ridiculous rumors. There's no such thing as ghosts."

His friend sighed. "I want to agree with you, obviously. At Keyvnor, there is the problem of multiple witnesses to multiple events. The word 'torment' is frequently used. Count yourself fortunate if you haven't seen them yet or felt their presence."

William looked hard at Blackwater. "Are you saying you've seen ghosts at Keyvnor?"

Blackwater looked up from his studied gaze at the floor to give William a quick, hard glance. "Have you not felt an icy chill in the air? Have you not heard things, felt things, that defied logic?"

William had, though he didn't want to admit it. "But...ghosts?"

He turned his gaze back to the floor, and said softly, "Thank God for Snow. His ring keeps them away."

"A ring?"

Blackwater shrugged. "Call it a Viking legend,

call it rubbish if you will. But whenever he's around, the apparitions leave. I've seen the ruby Grimstone glowing." He shrugged. "You must think I'm mad."

William was suddenly reminded of the card game the other night, when Marjorie had stared into the air behind him. There *had* been a chill in the room. Was it possible that she had cheated with the help of ghosts? The very idea was absurd, and he dismissed it. He ignored Blackwater's question and simply said, "Give my best to Lady Morgan, would you?"

With a nod, Blackwater departed.

William spent the next few hours wandering through the castle, trying to stay out of the way. It was the day before the wedding, and the castle was bustling with activity, though he had not seen Marjorie anywhere. Servants were busy decorating the Great Hall, while the kitchen staff began their preparations for the large Christmas Eve wedding feast tomorrow.

Outside, the sky was clear, and he decided to go walking. The brisk winter air might do him some good and take his mind off the wedding celebration. There were too many similarities to his own wedding a year ago, and it brought back all the memories he'd wanted to forget.

Like the bride never showing up.

It was unlikely that Laurie would attend, since she had not arrived thus far. And while William had wanted to prove that he had moved forward with his life, a part of him was glad that she was not here.

He strode through the gardens, noting that the clear skies had become slightly cloudy. He could see his breath in the air, and there was a heavy feeling of moisture. The wintry silence held its own spell of enchantment.

Just ahead, he saw Lady Marjorie. She wore a long red cloak with a hood, and upon one arm, she carried a basket. In her other hand, she held a pair of shears. At first, he thought she was walking into the garden, but then he realized she was headed toward the large garden maze.

He shouldn't follow her; he knew that. Yet he wondered why she had not sent a servant to fetch whatever it was she wanted. She should have brought a footman to escort her, at the very least, for protection. With so many unmarried gentlemen as wedding guests, it wasn't wise for a woman to go off on her own.

And so, he began trailing her to ensure her safety.

The maze was taller than him, and he could not see past the walls of greenery. It felt as if he were cloaked in winter, for the frigid air invaded his thin jacket. For a moment, he questioned the wisdom of entering a closed space. The last thing he wanted was to be trapped and surrounded by shrubbery. But neither did he want Lady Marjorie to be alone and unprotected.

He noticed that she had dropped a few holly berries along the path she had taken. Was the hedge maze so confusing that she felt the need to mark her way out? True, her father had only inherited the castle a few months ago, but surely she would know the way out by now.

William turned left and then right, trudging deeper among the hedges. Here and there were more holly berries scattered, their bright red color vivid against the dying winter grass.

The maze was indeed larger than he'd thought, with several twists and turns. Once or twice, he took a wrong direction but quickly found his way back because of the holly berries. Marjorie was indeed an intelligent woman to think of it. And yet, he wondered why she had come out to the garden alone.

Eventually, he caught up to her in the center of the maze. A large evergreen fir stood at one side, and she was reaching up to cut branches from it.

"Do you need help?" he asked.

She jerked at the sound of his voice. "You startled me, Sir William."

He almost smiled. "Why are you out cutting branches alone? Shouldn't you let a servant do that instead?"

"I wanted to escape the house," she admitted. "Everyone was running about, making preparations for the wedding. I needed some time to myself. My sisters are beside themselves with their wedding plans, and I thought this would be a good distraction." She set down her basket and regarded him. "Why did you follow me?"

"It's not safe for a woman to venture out alone. One of the guests might have bothered you."

"Such as yourself?" She raised an eyebrow at him. "I assure you, I am quite safe." To underscore her words, she raised the shears and demonstrated a snipping motion as if wielding a weapon.

"You are safe now," he corrected. "If you like, I can bend the branches down lower so you can cut them."

She shrugged. "Very well."

He drew closer and reached up to a higher branch on the fir tree. "How many do you need?"

"Just enough to fill the basket. Tamsyn wanted greenery to make garlands and wreaths for the house, so I offered to get some branches." She cut the limb he was holding and tucked it among the others at her feet. For a while, she worked in silence, and he was startled to realize how comfortable it was to be around her. Though she was normally quite talkative, today she seemed pensive.

He followed her toward another part of the maze where there was a large holly bush near a gazebo. Marjorie reached in with the shears and cut a branch, but let out a yelp after she pricked her finger. "Ouch. Those bushes are awful, even when you wear gloves." She stripped away the kid glove and rubbed at her bleeding fingertip.

"If you want to rest for a moment, I will cut the branches for you," he offered.

"That's kind of you." She pulled at the edges of her cloak. "I didn't think it would be this cold today. It almost feels like it might snow."

"It was clear enough when I followed you," he started to say, but then glanced upward. Above the maze, the skies had darkened and grown cloudy. All around them, the air seemed to freeze, and he rubbed at the shoulders of his jacket. He thought of Beck's suggestion of ghosts, but then dismissed the thought. It was weather, nothing more.

His prediction was proven right, for within moments, snow began falling swiftly. Marjorie hurried into the gazebo at the center of the maze, and he followed. She raised the hood of her red cloak and put her glove back on. "It looks as if I was right about the snow."

He said nothing, and as the snow fell harder, he felt foolish for being out of doors without a proper coat and hat. His impulse now meant great discomfort during this weather. Lady Marjorie eyed him and said, "You look cold."

"It's no matter. The storm will pass." He was not about to complain in front of her. It was a little snow, nothing more. It wasn't as if he would freeze to death. But the snow fell steadily, coating the ground.

"Here." Lady Marjorie reached for his ungloved hands and held them in hers. She brought them to the edge of her cloak and tried to cover them with the wool. The gesture of kindness startled him, for he hadn't expected it of her. Or from any woman, for that matter.

Certainly, when he'd encountered rainy weather with his former fiancée Laurie, she'd demanded that he remove his coat and hold it over her head. In contrast, it seemed that Lady Marjorie would have offered to share her cloak, were it not so improper.

Beneath the wool, her hands warmed his. It meant nothing, he knew—and yet, he felt the hard edges of his bitterness beginning to soften. She was offering friendship, and for a moment, he didn't yearn for isolation. Her presence was almost... comforting.

Marjorie ventured a tentative smile. "We should leave the maze before you're transformed into a snowman."

William nodded because it was expected of him. And yet, he didn't hurry away from the gazebo. He was enjoying her presence while the snow fell around them.

Once they left the shelter, snowflakes dotted her lashes and cheeks. She was smiling as the storm died down and faded away. They passed by a hazel tree, and a gust of wind blew across the branches, showering snow over Marjorie. She laughed, brushing away the white flakes from her red cloak. "It looks as if I've been given another gown, doesn't it?"

As they trudged back through the maze, the ground was now lightly covered with snow. Marjorie's good mood sobered. "I can't see the holly berries to find our way back." With a wry smile, she added, "I thought it was a good idea at the time."

"We'll find the way," he promised. "It won't take long, now that the snow has stopped."

William kicked at the snowy pathway, hoping to unearth the berries, but there were none to be found. He followed her through the maze, but she was not going back the way they had come. "Shouldn't we have turned that way?" he ventured.

She lifted her hands in defeat. "Why do you think I used the berries to mark my path? I've only lived here since October. I don't know this maze at all."

"You needn't be afraid," he reassured her. "It can't be far."

"That's not what worries me." She slowed her pace, kicking at the slight layer of snow on the ground. "No one can find out that we were alone together in the maze. If they do, they might think that you—that we—" Her words broke off, and she flushed. "Let us just say that I do not wish to be forced into marriage."

"Especially with a man like me," he finished. Her meaning was clear enough, though he knew what she thought of him.

"With any man," she corrected. "I do not wish to be married any more than you do."

He was intrigued, for most women *did* want marriage. "Why not?"

A lock of her strawberry blond hair fell from her red hood, and she tried to tuck it back. Her brown eyes held frustration, but he found himself noticing her more. Her beauty was unusual, like an autumn leaf with unexpected colors.

Her lips tightened into a line. "Let us simply say that my last suitor believed that I should obey his every command without question. I had no freedom at all."

She didn't elaborate any more, but picked up her skirts to hurry through the maze. He followed, but when she rounded another corner, she stumbled backwards, nearly crashing into him. Her expression held panic, and her coloring had gone pale. "We can't go that way, Sir William."

He stared at the path, which seemed to lead toward the house. "Why not? I think it's the way back."

She shook her head. "There's another way out. I found it by accident in November. We should try to find it."

He took her by the hand. "Lady Marjorie, this *is* the way. I know it is."

She jolted at his tone and pulled her hand away. There was a strange expression on her face, as if he'd said something amiss. Before he could ask what was wrong, she hurried in another direction. He couldn't understand what had frightened her, but it almost seemed as if she had seen something.

Something she didn't want him to know about.

He saw no choice but to follow.

※

Marjorie's heart was pounding as if a thousand demons were chasing her. While many of Castle Keyvnor's ghosts were harmless, she didn't trust the Man in Black. They'd suspected he was a pirate in life, and when she had seen him in the maze just now, he'd held a gleaming blade in his hand. While she didn't know if a specter's weapon held any corporeal power, she wasn't about to chance it—no matter how much Sir William insisted that it was the right path.

His sudden commanding tone bothered her, for it reminded her of Lord Dewbury's nature. For a moment, she'd been afraid he would ignore her wishes and take her hand, leading her straight into danger.

She wasn't about to take that risk, and that was why she'd pulled free of his hand and had run from both of them. Marjorie hardly cared where she was going, but fear led her past the hedge rows and into a dead end. She stopped running and turned around, only to see William waiting for her.

"Something frightened you back there."

Marjorie nodded but didn't elaborate. He would think she was losing her wits, and she wasn't about to admit the truth—that she was seeing ghosts. She closed her eyes, trying to calm her racing heart.

He paused a moment. "And you won't tell me why you started running away from that part of the maze?" This time his voice was gentle, almost concerned.

She shook her head. At that, he folded his arms and regarded her. "Earlier, you accused me of being too quiet. Now it seems that you've become the taciturn one."

"Not a habit, I assure you." But the ghosts at Castle Keyvnor were real—she had seen them every day since her arrival here. Some were kindly, but others terrified her—especially the Man in Black.

"We need to find the way out," she murmured.

He offered his arm. "We will. I promise you that." This time, he took a step in the opposite direction from the ghost, and she tried to calm her racing heart. William's presence lent her comfort, and she was grateful that he was here. The last thing she wanted was to be cornered alone with a ghost.

"Thank goodness for that." She took his arm and he rested his gloved hand upon hers. The light heat of his touch startled her, and though it was only meant as reassurance, the slight pressure made her cheeks flush. Marjorie adjusted the basket on her opposite arm, only to realize that she had scattered several of the branches on the melting snow during her hasty retreat.

Sir William helped her to pick them up again, and he asked, "Where do you think we'll find the other way out of the maze?"

"I think I could find it if we return to the gazebo." She walked back with him and thankfully saw no more ghosts. "I believe it's this pathway."

Sir William led her away from the part of the maze where she'd been frightened and back toward the center. As they passed the gazebo, he remarked, "Did you notice that there was hardly any snow on the ground on the opposite side of that hedgerow?"

"I wasn't paying attention." Because she was too busy being terrorized by a ghost.

"It was almost as if it only snowed inside the maze. But that's impossible."

Nothing was impossible when meddling ghosts were involved. Their very presence dropped the temperature quite a bit—and Marjorie wouldn't put it past them to conjure snow. She pointed toward the north end of the gazebo and said, "Let's try that pathway."

Sir William accompanied her, and they turned another corner. For a time, they walked in silence, but she was conscious of his strength. He wore only his jacket, and it was entirely too thin for the weather. Yet he had made no complaint at all.

"I think we've found the way out," he said at last. "Which is most fortunate, since I should hate to die of starvation, lost in this maze."

He reached out and lifted her fallen red hood over her hair. The gesture was kind, and a sudden flush came over her cheeks. Marjorie walked alongside him toward the opening in the hedge. The moment she stepped through it, she saw dying grass beneath her feet without a trace of snow. Strange indeed.

They emerged from the hedgerow maze and found themselves near the kitchens. In addition to the main kitchens, the castle had an outside building that had been used hundreds of years ago, to prevent fire from reaching the main keep. Delicious aromas scented the air, luring them closer.

"Is that gingerbread?" Marjorie wondered aloud, eyeing the kitchen.

A boyish smile slid over William's face. "I, for one, am starving. We should go and find out what it is. And better, if they have any scraps to share."

CHAPTER THREE

They hurried toward the outbuilding, which was constructed of rough limestone. Smoke swirled from the brick chimney, and her stomach rumbled when they drew closer. "I'm hungry enough to eat the house," Marjorie admitted.

Sir William opened the door for her, and the heat from the kitchen hearth was a blessed relief. Marjorie froze at the sight of food before them, and it was all she could do not to throw herself at the table of sweets. Several layer cakes were filled with dried fruit and soaked in brandy. The cook, Mrs. Woodbead, had also made dozens of mince pies, sugared almonds, and gingerbread dotted with currants.

Sir William cast a sidelong glance at the table. "This gingerbread appears slightly burned."

Marjorie understood exactly what he was

implying. "Cook cannot serve that at the wedding feast. It would be a bad reflection of her skills." She glanced around and saw no one. And truthfully, she *was* the daughter of Lord Banfield. It was not as if she couldn't help herself to the gingerbread, since she lived here.

She found a wooden spoon and handed it to Sir William and then chose another for herself. There was a small container of clotted cream, and she offered it to him. "Would you like cream with your gingerbread?"

"Pour it over the entire cake," he suggested.

She did, never minding that the cake was still warm. They pulled up stools beside the kitchen table and devoured the gingerbread with their spoons. For a time, it was as if they were children, sneaking sweets when no one was around. The cream was delicious upon the hot spiced gingerbread cake, and she took an enormous spoonful.

"I don't care that it's burned. I do love this." She wiped at a bit of the cream on her lip, smiling at him.

Sir William slid his spoon into the gingerbread and devoured his portion. "You like dessert, don't you?"

She nodded. "Very much, though I am not supposed to have it very often."

He shrugged. "There's no harm in enjoying cake, is there?"

"There was a time when I was not permitted to have it at all," she confessed.

In answer, he pushed a generous spoonful toward her. "Did your parents forbid it?"

"No, it was…someone else." She wasn't at all certain she wanted to admit the truth to Sir William, though many people knew she had been engaged to Viscount Dewbury. To distract herself, she ate the gingerbread.

He frowned, as if trying to discern the truth. His blue eyes seemed to drink in her features, and her face warmed with a sudden flush. She realized that she was enjoying herself in his presence.

She liked Sir William very much—perhaps too much. It was better not to let her feelings wander past friendship. Her sisters would be married tomorrow, and he would leave soon afterward. The thought was strangely disturbing. It shouldn't matter, and yet…it did somehow. If she didn't gather command of her senses, she might make an idiot of herself.

Like all men, he will tell you what to do. He will seize control of your life, and you will have no freedom of your own. She had to recognize the risks and protect herself from falling into the trap of romance.

"You're staring at me," he remarked.

"I'm sorry." She grasped for an excuse and saw a bit of cream on his upper lip. "You have something on your mouth, just there."

His expression turned to one of interest. He reached for her ungloved hand and drew it toward his face. "Show me."

His cheek was warm beneath her palm and clean-shaven. She was fascinated by the hard planes of his face and traced the edge of his jaw, before wiping at an imaginary place above his mouth. "I think that's it."

Her voice came out as a whisper, and he caught her hand and held it to his face. For a moment, she remained frozen, knowing she should pull away—and yet not wanting to.

"I think you have something on your mouth as well." He reached out and cupped her face in his hands. His thumb stroked down the edge of her cheek, ending at her mouth.

She didn't move, didn't speak. Her heart was pounding, and he gave her every opportunity to pull back before he leaned in to kiss her.

His mouth was warm, an offering that slid past the edges of friendship, inviting her toward something more. She tasted the gingerbread upon his mouth, and it felt as if he were devouring her.

Her body warmed to his, and she surrendered to the kiss, despite her own inhibitions.

Don't do this, her mind warned.

But her body ignored common sense, and she realized that she was kissing him back. It was wrong to indulge in this moment, but a part of her reveled in the unexpected affection.

A blast of frigid air made her break away from him, shocking her back into reality. The kitchen door was flung open, and a moment later, she heard a female voice screech, "Who is eating my cakes?"

Marjorie turned and saw an older woman with gray hair, wearing a black dress. She had never seen the servant before. "Who are you?"

"I am Mrs. Hechs. I was hired to help the cook with all the food for the wedding feast." She hobbled toward them and placed her hands akimbo. "Were you that hungry, *dear*?"

She spoke the word *dear* in the same tone as if calling her a horrid creature. But Marjorie refused to be cowed. "The gingerbread cake was burned, and we were hungry. It wasn't fit to serve to anyone."

Her words seemed to incite a vicious anger in the older woman. Mrs. Hechs glared at her as if she wanted to set her on fire. Instead, she held her tongue and turned back to Sir William.

"That cake was for the wedding tomorrow," she said coolly. "Though I see *you* could stand to be fattened up, sir. You look as if your family denied you any food."

The woman's acerbic nature startled Marjorie. She was about to chide the woman, but William interrupted, "I assure you, they did not." Then he continued, attempting to soften her temper. "The cake was delicious, however. My compliments on your cooking." It was clear he was trying to soften the woman's anger, and it seemed to work.

Mrs. Hechs smiled at him. "I have other cakes and a boiled pudding with a delicious brandy sauce you might enjoy," she said, in an inviting tone. "They are stored in the pantry for now. Would you like to see them?"

Was the cook *flirting* with him? Marjorie's gaze narrowed, but she found her own amusement in Sir William's discomfort.

"I think it's time that I returned to the house. But thank you."

"Oh, but I must insist." She reached out to touch his hand, but William flinched and backed away. "At least come inside and tell me what you think of the sweets." The old woman opened the pantry door and beamed at him.

"Another time, perhaps, Mrs. Hechs."

The cook batted her lashes. "Do you know, you are quite a handsome man. If I were twenty years younger, I could eat you up."

It was all Marjorie could do not to laugh. William looked as if he were trying to maintain a straight face, but his eyes held horror.

"Come inside and have a taste," she invited. Marjorie followed, but a sharp look from Mrs. Hechs reminded her that she was not invited to partake in the sweets. Which was odd, really, since her father paid the woman's wages. Instead, Marjorie remained at the doorway of the pantry, a slight smile on her face. Sir William was clearly cornered, though he tried to make polite compliments about the boiled pudding with the holly sprig on top.

"Shouldn't you be preparing a tray for tea?" Marjorie suggested. "We have dozens of hungry guests. Sir William and I can leave you to it."

It was clear that Mrs. Hechs did not want to leave. She shot the pair of them a look and then wiped her hands on her apron and seized a tray containing four spice cakes. "Do not eat anything else until I return," she warned.

When the old woman had gone, Sir William asked, "Was it me, or did her behavior seem strange somehow?"

Marjorie shook her head. "I have no idea. Don't

pay her any heed." But she thought of mentioning the new cook's behavior to her mother. It was quite strange indeed. And where was Mrs. Woodbead?

Sir William reached toward one of the trays and picked up a sugared plum. "I am sorry if I overstepped earlier, when I kissed you. It was an impulse."

Marjorie's cheeks burned, and she took another step into the pantry, feeling uncertain about what to say. Should she be honest? Should she tell him never to do it again? She could hardly find any words at all to speak. The kiss had startled her, but she had enjoyed it. In fact, she rather wanted to be kissed again—especially since she might not see him again after he departed. Without knowing why, she lifted her chin and murmured, "I am not sorry."

She couldn't understand the sudden yearning within her. William drew closer, and she backed into one of the shelves. He rested both hands on the shelf behind her, and she could feel the length of his body pressed close. "I liked kissing you, too. You are a beautiful woman, Lady Marjorie."

"I shouldn't be here with you," she murmured. "Neither of us is looking for marriage."

But her hands moved up to rest upon his cravat. It was the only invitation he needed, and this time, he claimed her mouth with a reckless abandon. He kissed her as if he wanted no other woman in the world, and she yielded to him, reveling in the fire that rose between them. She wound her arms around his neck and surrendered to the kiss. His tongue slid inside, and she moaned, feeling the echo of sensation between her thighs. Never before had she felt such desire—she hadn't known it existed. Lord Dewbury had only kissed her hand, and even then, it had evoked no reaction at all.

With William, the kiss was like a forbidden sweet—and she enjoyed it without fearing the consequences.

His mouth moved from her lips to her cheek, nibbling at her neck. "You're making me lose myself. And I find that I don't care."

Shivers erupted across her skin, and her breasts tightened against her chemise. Her body was so sensitive to his touch, she felt as if she were taut with need.

"I've never been kissed like this before," she admitted. "It's almost frightening."

At that, he pulled back, nipping at her lips one last time. "That wasn't my intention." He stepped back and then drew her out of the pantry.

A sudden breeze swept into the kitchen, and Marjorie felt the chill beneath her red cloak, freezing the very air. She tensed, for in the past, a sudden gust of frigid air meant that one of the castle ghosts was nearby. But this time, she could see nothing.

"We should go back inside the castle," she told him.

William was staring at something behind her, and his own expression transformed. "I agree."

She took his arm and started to walk toward the door, but he paused a moment. "Wait, Lady Marjorie."

The air was so frigid, she already knew what he was seeing—one of the ghosts. "We have to leave, Sir William. It's so cold in here."

But the moment she took a step forward, an unseen presence slammed against her shoulders. It was like a wall of ice throwing her backwards, and she gasped as she lost her balance. She was falling toward the kitchen hearth, where the fire burned brightly. Marjorie tried to right herself, but the ghostly presence shoved her back. She nearly tumbled into the fire, but William seized her waist and jerked her back again.

And then she saw Mrs. Hechs, who had returned to the threshold.

"Were you trying to eat my cakes again?" The woman's tone was menacing, and she advanced toward them. Her voice grew louder, and in that moment, she reminded Marjorie of a witch. "I told you not to touch them! Get away!" She rose from the ground, and her features grew more transparent.

There was a young maid standing at the door behind her. Sir William caught sight of her and demanded, "Fetch Lord Snowingham. Now!"

The girl dropped her tray, fleeing the kitchen. More than anything, Marjorie wished she could do the same, but it was all she could do to fight against the invisible hands pushing her backwards. Now, it was becoming clear—Mrs. Hechs was not, in fact, an extra cook hired to help with preparing food for her sisters' weddings. She was something far worse—a castle ghost with the power to cause true mischief.

And now, she understood why Sir William had summoned Lord Snowingham. There were rumors that Lord Snow possessed the power to repel ghosts because of an ancient Viking ring he had inherited. Some had claimed that the Grimstone ruby glowed in the presence of spirits. She didn't know if that was true or not, but any help at all was welcome now. She met William's gaze, and there was a silent exchange between them. "We will leave now, Mrs. Hechs. I am sorry we ate your gingerbread cake."

"You won't be going anywhere!" the ghost shrieked, and Marjorie ducked when one of the pans came flying toward her head.

William seized a cast iron skillet and used it as a shield, taking Marjorie by the hand. Mrs. Hechs grew enraged, and another frigid blast of air knocked Marjorie to the ground. Each time she tried to stand, the ghost shoved her closer to the hearth fire. Sir William dropped the skillet and helped her to stand, gripping her hand tightly. "Let's go."

Marjorie felt the frigid air swirling around them, but William used his strength to keep her away from the fire. He took one step toward the door, then another. Behind them, the flames rose hotter, as if Mrs. Hechs were stoking them.

Marjorie held on tighter to Sir William, as if to hold back the ghost's power. When another gust of frigid air knocked against them, Sir William lost his balance. Marjorie fell on the floor and seized a linen towel, using it to pick up a hot poker near the hearth. No longer would she remain this ghost's victim—not now. She used both hands to wield it against Mrs. Hechs.

"I will *not* be threatened in my father's house," she insisted. "Ghost or not." She wasn't entirely certain what she would do with the hot poker, but as she neared Mrs. Hechs, steam rose within the air, and hot water dripped down the iron rod. The ghost backed away from the fiery poker, and William seized the shovel beside the hearth, joining her in the fight. They had nearly reached the doorway when suddenly, there came a loud crack of thunder and the ghost abruptly vanished. Lord Snowingham stood a few feet away, shadowed by the terrified maid.

His gaze turned somber, and he asked, "Are you all right, Lady Marjorie? And you, Sir William?"

She nodded. "I've never seen that ghost before. She was pretending to be the cook."

Lord Snowingham rubbed at the glowing ruby ring upon his right index finger. Marjorie hadn't truly believed that the Grimstone could drive away ghosts…until now.

Snowingham continued, "The kitchen maid came to fetch me when she saw—"

"—Mrs. Hechs, yes," Marjorie finished. "Thank goodness she's gone." Her heart was still pounding from the encounter, and she was grateful that the earl had come.

"I am glad you are unharmed," Snowingham finished. "What of you, Sir William?"

He set down the shovel and let out a slow breath. "I never really believed in ghosts before. But this castle is quite…unusual, I must say."

"You look as if you could use a brandy," the earl remarked. "Shall we go?"

Marjorie glanced behind her and took one of the

boiled puddings soaked in brandy, placing it on a small plate. Since her mother would never permit a lady to indulge in spirits, it would have to do. Then she located her basket of greenery and looped it over her right arm.

Sir William helped her with the small plate. "I believe we should all share the pudding, along with some brandy. It has been a terrible afternoon, don't you think?"

Not as terrible as it could have been, had she been alone in the kitchens. They continued walking toward the castle, and along the way, Marjorie spied a handful of holly berries, leading toward one of the castle doors.

"Did you drop those?" Sir William inquired.

"No. And after what we've just endured, I would suggest that we don't follow that pathway." She smiled and they returned to the stairs leading to the back door. From behind her, there came a frigid gust of wind, as if another ghost was trailing them.

Marjorie stiffened her shoulders and ignored it, refusing to look back.

༄

William was only too glad to get away from the kitchen, in search of a quiet room and a brandy.

When they entered the castle, Lord Snowingham was about to join them in the parlor, when he suddenly caught sight of Marjorie's sister, Rose. "Forgive me, but I suddenly remembered a prior engagement."

Marjorie's face stiffened, but she murmured a polite farewell. Once he had left, William asked, "Is something wrong?"

"No, not really. But did you see his face?" She strode into the sitting room, and set the pudding down upon a small table. Then she sank into a chair and rang for a servant. "He is fascinated by my sister. I cannot believe it."

"Didn't they meet only a few days ago?" William kept his tone relaxed, but his own mood tightened. He had shielded his emotions, revealing no response to the past hour. Yet inwardly, he'd been shaken by what he had witnessed. He had never seen a ghost before in his life, much less one with the power to do harm.

Even more unnerving was his reaction to the danger. He had fought to save Marjorie, and even now, energy coursed through his veins. He felt the need to release the tension in some way, but there was no means to do so. Sometimes, he went riding when he was restless, but there were far too many guests to make that possible.

"I cannot imagine falling in love with someone I only just met," she remarked. When the footman arrived, she ordered brandy for William and tea for herself. Then she thought a moment and stood from her chair. "I wonder if they are still there. Perhaps Rose might wish to join us." She went to stand at the door, and William joined her, peering over her shoulder. At the end of the hall, Lady Rose smiled up at Lord Snow, and he held her hands in his.

"He looks quite taken with her." William stood so close to Marjorie, he could smell the scent of flowers in her hair, and the barest hint of gingerbread. Her back was pressed to him, and he found himself wanting to pull her into his arms and kiss her again. It was as if he were caught under an enchantment, needing to taste her lips again. If this was indeed a spell, he wasn't certain if he wanted anyone to break it.

"He does," Marjorie lamented.

"Why does that upset you? Don't you want your sister to be happy?"

"I do." But her voice sounded sad. He waited for her to elaborate, and she added, "I'm just a selfish woman who doesn't want to be left alone. Tamsyn and Morgan are getting married. And now Rose and Gwyn are husband-hunting. I know it's terrible of me, but it feels as if our family is breaking apart."

"It might not be as bad as you think." It was the only thing he could think of to say, but he knew all about relationships falling into pieces.

Marjorie turned abruptly, and he realized he had his arms around her. She cleared her throat, and he released her immediately. "Sorry."

Two footmen arrived with tea and brandy, along with a second plate and two silver forks for the pudding. "Shall I send for your mother, Lady Marjorie?" He gave a pointed glance at William in a reminder that they both needed a chaperone.

"No, she will be immersed in wedding plans. Ask Lady Octavia if she will come to chaperone," she countered. "And bring another fork for her, in case she wishes to share the pudding."

After the two footmen had left, William regarded her. "Are you afraid of others talking about us?"

Marjorie shook her head, but he didn't miss the blush on her cheeks. "We won't be left alone for very long. And besides that, anyone could walk in. There's nothing wrong with having tea."

He lowered his voice. "But when our chaperone arrives, I won't be able to kiss you the way I want to."

Her face turned scarlet, and she took a fork from the tray and dug it into the pudding as a distraction. "We won't speak of that again. It shouldn't have happened."

"But it did. And can you deny that you enjoyed it?"

She ate a bite of the pudding to avoid answering his question. "Today was a trying day, one that I still don't understand. What happened in the kitchens with that ghost was awful, and I don't want to think of it."

He passed the brandy to her, offering to share the drink. Marjorie glanced around and then took the glass, taking the tiniest sip. She winced and took a breath. "Goodness, that *is* strong."

He took the glass back, swallowing more brandy without taking his eyes off her. She slid the fork into her mouth and closed her eyes again while she chewed. Whenever she ate sweets, Marjorie looked like a woman about to tumble into a lover's arms.

"Are your sisters eager to be married?" he asked.

Marjorie's face softened. "Both Tamsyn and Morgan love their husbands to be. I am happy for both of them."

"But you still have no wish to marry?" He wondered if some gentleman had broken her heart years ago.

She shook her head. "I have no wish to be imprisoned within matrimony. Not when it means becoming a man's puppet, where he tries to control my every word and deed."

It was a strange thing to say, but before he could ask her more, she gave a rueful smile. "As I told you earlier, I would marry cake, if I could." She took another bite, and then poured herself tea. "To be honest, I know that most men want control of my dowry and not much else."

She cast a sidelong glance at him, but William said nothing. He only had a lesser title, and likely she believed he was a fortune hunter like other gentlemen. Most women overlooked him for that reason, never dreaming that he had wealth of his own. Laurie had been the exception, until she had changed her mind on their wedding day.

He reached for his own fork and dug into the pudding. The heavy scent of spices, mingled with rum and dried fruit, was intoxicating. After the first bite, he took another, larger portion.

"Don't eat it all," Marjorie warned. "Save some for me."

He rather liked a challenge, so he reached with his fork, only to be blocked by Marjorie's fork. A sly smile came over her face, and she held it like a rapier. "*En garde.*"

"Sword fighting with a fork, Lady Marjorie?"

"I'm merely protecting my best interests." She clanged her silver fork against his, and he parried the blow with his own, biting back a laugh.

Marjorie was amusing in a way he'd never expected, and their forks clashed, over and over. When at last she locked forks with his, he reached out with his other hand and broke off a hunk of the pudding.

"Cheating knave," she accused.

He bit off a piece of the pudding and then reached out to put the rest in her mouth. "I'll share." His thumb brushed against her silken lips, and she suddenly went quite still.

Though she ate the pudding, her brown eyes held uncertainty. William cupped her cheek, tracing the delicate line of her jaw. Those lips tempted him to pull her nearer, to taste her once more.

And though he knew it was too forward, he gave in to the urge.

He captured her mouth, kissing her deeply. There was something about Lady Marjorie that made it impossible to stop with only a kiss. He didn't care about the consequences just now, only enjoying the softness of her mouth and her hands resting upon his shoulders.

He pulled back, wondering if she felt the same way he did. Her eyes were bright, and her lips red. And yet she wasn't pushing him away.

"Sir William, we shouldn't—" Marjorie began.

He ignored her and kissed her again, this time

sliding his tongue against the seam of her lips. She yielded to him, welcoming him inside. There was the tentative answer of her own tongue, and she wound her arms around his neck.

Heat roared through him. The very idea of this liaison was forbidden, but he craved her deeply.

A slight gasp interrupted the kiss, and he broke away, only to see Ariadne Cushing standing at the door. Her face had gone white, and she demanded, "Were you laughing at me, all this time?"

"Ariadne, no. I'm sorry—this isn't what you think. We didn't mean to—" Marjorie stood, clutching her hands together, her expression pained. "No one was laughing at you."

"You said you would help me, Cousin Marjorie. But now, I think both of you were scheming, only to make a fool of me." The young woman's face held humiliation, and she closed her eyes. "I suppose it serves me right to think that any man would want someone like me."

"You're wrong," Marjorie insisted. "And I *am* sorry for this. I never meant for it to happen."

"Your footman asked me to come as a chaperone, since Lady Octavia was not here. And then I find you kissing the man you were trying to match with me?" She shook her head and took a step backward. "I never thought you would behave in such a despicable way, Marjorie. I thought you would help me, not betray me."

William didn't want to stand by and say nothing, so he intervened, "I am sorry for all of this, Miss Cushing. But I do not think we would have been suited to one another, and I blame myself for not being honest from the first. If you would prefer an introduction to another gentleman, I could try to help."

"The last thing I want is help from either one of you," she fired back before she strode out of the room.

Marjorie's face was pale, and she kept her hands clenched together. "I never meant to hurt her like this."

He didn't know what to say or do, for he was responsible for embarrassing the young woman when he hadn't meant to. "There may be a few of my friends who might be interested in speaking with her."

She pushed aside her teacup. "I need to apologize to her. I feel terrible that this happened."

He disagreed and took her hand. "I don't feel terrible for kissing you, Lady Marjorie." To the contrary, he had enjoyed being with her.

A broken smile twisted her face. "But where can it lead? Neither of us wants marriage." She stood from her chair and faced him. "I think it's best if we end it right now and remain only friends, Sir William."

The sadness in her eyes took him aback, for her mood seemed to belie her words. But there was nothing more to say, was there?

Without waiting for a reply, she walked out of the room.

Chapter Four

It was the morning of her sisters' weddings, and Marjorie had barely slept at all. Castle Keyvnor had been decorated beautifully, with swags of greenery and green wreaths on every door. Cheerful red and white ribbons were hung here and there, and holly branches adorned the fireplace mantel. Marjorie also spied sprigs of mistletoe in hidden corners.

Which was probably Gwyn's doing, for her sister was a true romantic.

After she counted the fifth sprig, a blush spread over her cheeks. The very thought of kissing turned her insides into custard. How could she have ever thought Sir William was a boring, quiet man? His kisses had turned her inside out, and she secretly craved more.

She wore a light green gown trimmed with lace, and her maid had arranged a cluster of holly in her hair, the thorns shielded by red ribbons. Gwyn had arranged for the decoration, insisting that she wear it for the wedding.

Her sisters were almost giddy with joy this morning, and a knot formed in her stomach. They both acted like women in love, and soon enough, Marjorie would be left alone. The thought evoked an ache in her heart, for she could not imagine an empty household without her sisters.

A few guests had arrived only this morning, just in time for the wedding. Her mother had greeted them, but Marjorie had paid little attention to the newcomers.

Until she heard Ariadne approaching. She was about to apologize, when her cousin interrupted. "Did you know that Sir William's fiancée is here?"

She frowned, not understanding. "He isn't engaged to anyone, Ariadne."

Her cousin's face tightened. "Oh, but he was last Christmas. And she's here now. Just look."

Marjorie wasn't certain who Ariadne was talking about, but she turned toward the group of guests and saw a beautiful blond-haired woman wearing a dress the color of a delicate pink rose. The wedding had not yet begun, and the woman crossed through the dozens of guests until she stood before Sir William.

The emotions on his face shifted from shock, to longing, to anger. But there was no surprise on his face, and when the woman reached out to touch his arm, he didn't pull away.

Marjorie felt as if she'd taken a fist to the gut. Sir William had said that he didn't want to be married, but he had never mentioned that he had once been engaged. She should have expected it.

And if it had happened during Christmas last year, it explained his reasons for not liking the holiday. She pushed back the emotions rising within her and murmured to Ariadne, "Who is she?"

"Her name is Laurie Kent. And from what I understand, she left him because she didn't want to marry a pauper." Ariadne's anger seemed to soften, and she let out a sigh. "I suppose it's better that Sir William didn't want someone like me. And now that Miss Kent has returned…" She let her words trail off, knowing that Marjorie would predict her meaning.

Her gaze sharpened upon them, and she suppressed the unwanted flare of jealousy. It shouldn't matter if he saw Miss Kent or even if he reunited with the woman he had once loved. Why should she care if he did? They were friends, nothing more. Marjorie tried to tell herself that he could do as he pleased, but inwardly, she felt an unexpected sense of loss.

Yesterday had been a troubling day, one that had filled her with uncertainty. She could not deny that she was attracted to William or that she had enjoyed every kiss. Even now, her feelings were bruised and downtrodden, for she was beginning to understand why he refused to consider marriage—if he was still in love with someone else. The kiss had been an impulse, just as he'd said. He might have been toying with her, pushing the boundaries of propriety…and she had fallen into that trap.

Marjorie took her place beside her mother as the wedding began, and when she saw her sisters gazing into the eyes of their bridegrooms, her heart constricted. This was what love looked like. Morgan smiled up at Hal as if he was the man of her dreams. And Tamsyn gazed into Gryffyn's eyes as if she could not wait to become his wife.

Marjorie searched the crowd of people until she caught sight of Miss Kent. The young woman dabbed at her eyes with a handkerchief, and she stared at Sir William, whose eyes were fixed upon the clergyman.

Had he ever kissed Miss Kent in the way he'd kissed her? Surely, he had.

Again, she berated herself for even thinking of it. His past didn't matter, and they had no future together. They would not sit across the table from one another, dueling with forks. They would not steal Christmas puddings from the kitchen or play cards against one another.

A heaviness cloaked her emotions, for she hadn't thought it was possible to have strong feelings for a man—not this soon.

She joined the guests in applauding when the wedding was over and her sisters had kissed their new husbands. Beside her, Lady Banfield wiped her eyes with a handkerchief, smiling through her tears of joy. Marjorie hugged each of her sisters, wishing them happiness, and she truly did want that. Tamsyn and Morgan were both very dear to her, and she sincerely wanted the best for them.

While the other guests stood in line to wish them well, Marjorie slipped out of the Great Hall and found a quiet corner. She took comfort in the quiet and told herself that she had done the right thing, telling Sir William that there could be nothing more between them. Especially if he cared for someone else.

But when she saw him walk into the corridor, Marjorie ducked behind the staircase, not wanting him to see her. Just as she'd feared, Miss Kent followed him. It wasn't right to eavesdrop, and Marjorie knew she ought to step out of the shadows, but curiosity kept her there.

"You look well, William," Miss Kent said softly.

"I am glad to see you once again."

He didn't answer, and Marjorie felt a slight sense of satisfaction that the brooding, silent man was back. Good. If Miss Kent had abandoned him at the altar, she deserved that.

"I didn't realize you knew Lord and Lady Banfield," Miss Kent continued. She drew closer to Sir William, who took a step back.

Marjorie peered through the banister and saw the grim expression on his face. "Why are you here, Laurie?" he demanded.

She appeared taken aback. "I was invited to the wedding. And when I learned you were attending, I… I hoped to see you again."

"For what purpose?" His voice was rigid, and Marjorie sensed the anger and pain within it. She couldn't help but share his sentiments.

"To apologize," she said quietly. "I was wrong to leave you the way I did. It wasn't fair, and it wasn't right."

Silence again. Marjorie was secretly glad of it, and she waited for him to tell Miss Kent to go away. He didn't. Instead, he said quietly, "I accept your apology."

What? Was he simply going to open his arms to this woman and let go of the past? She nearly blinked at that.

Miss Kent's smile was stunning, and she took his hands in hers. "I am so glad to hear you say this. I wanted to atone for my mistakes and start again."

He leaned in, and Marjorie couldn't hear what he said. But within a moment, Miss Kent squeezed his hands and smiled before she departed to mingle among the guests.

Rubbish. She'd hoped to find out what was happening, even if that did make her a busybody.

But she wasn't expecting Sir William to clear his throat and say, "You can come out now, Lady Marjorie."

Color flooded her cheeks, but she obeyed. He was watching her with a knowing look, as if he'd been aware she was in hiding. "Spying on me, were you?"

"To be fair, I was enjoying a quiet corner when the pair of you came along. I didn't want to interrupt your conversation."

"Because you were spying."

"Not exactly. But I didn't want to spoil your moment together."

He leaned up against the staircase and sent her a knowing look. "Miss Kent and I were engaged to be married, nearly a year ago."

"I suppose that's why you despise Christmas, isn't it?"

"It's not my favorite holiday." He cast another look toward her. "What else did you want to know? That she broke our engagement and fled the wedding, with no explanation?"

"Cousin Ariadne told me she left you because you were a pauper."

An odd expression slid over his face. "She never said why she left. She only left a note that she no longer wished to marry me." He moved to stand beside her then, in the shadows. "I suppose we would not have made a good marriage, after all."

Perhaps it wasn't very nice, but Marjorie was rather glad of that. "If my cousin is right, and she walked away from you because she was afraid of poverty, you're well rid of her."

"Wouldn't you be?" he countered.

"I never had to worry about money, to be honest." Her father's wealth had meant that it was never a concern. Her dowry had lured Viscount Dewbury, and if she wanted to find another man to wed, it would not be difficult. Which she didn't.

Then she turned back to him and remarked, "You never told me about Miss Kent."

"You never told me about anyone from your past, either," he pointed out. "Does it matter?"

She wanted to say no, but she couldn't quite bring herself to speak. For he was right. She had never once mentioned Lord Dewbury to him. Should she? But then again, her mistakes were better forgotten. "No," she said quietly. "I suppose the past doesn't matter at all."

Sir William moved in closer. "Not anymore."

Her skin tightened at his presence, yearning for him once again. She fumbled for something to stay, anything to distract herself from the feelings she didn't want to face. "You didn't deserve what Miss Kent did to you. If she had second thoughts about the marriage, she should have told you far earlier. Waiting until the day of the wedding is simply abominable." She knew that her tone was far too critical, but she couldn't stop herself from adding, "You should have given her the cut direct."

"I was curious as to why she wanted to speak with me. And as I told you before, she is the reason I came to this wedding. I wanted to face her, so she would know that I have moved on with my life."

But she wasn't certain that was true, since he never intended to marry again. She ventured, "I don't understand how you can forgive her so easily."

"Because I am a saint," he said drily, and at that, she laughed aloud.

"No, Sir William, you are anything but a saint." He was the sort of man who would pull her into a dark corner and kiss her until her knees grew weak. And she had to admit to herself that she liked him entirely too much. He made her *want* to seek out dark corners.

Dozens of guests poured from the Great Hall at that moment, and she had no choice but to greet distant family members and friends. She saw her sister Rose speaking with Lord Snowingham, and even Gwyn was talking to Pendarvis.

"Save a dance for me this evening at the Yule Ball," he said quietly. Then he squeezed her hand and left her side.

Marjorie couldn't give an answer, for she was uncertain of where her feelings lay. Whenever she was with him, it seemed as if the rest of the world fell away, leaving them alone. She was far too attracted to this man, wanting to rest her cheek against his chest while he held her.

William unsettled her, for she didn't want to care for him. Yet, the moment she had seen Miss Kent making eyes at him, she couldn't stop the surge of jealousy. Which was so very odd.

A cold sensation drifted over her shoulders, and she stopped walking. Glaring into the shadows, she snapped, "That's quite enough. Leave me alone, or I'll bring Lord Snowingham to blast you into the hereafter."

Instantly the cold vanished, and she saw the ghost of Benedict drifting away. Her mood softened, for she rather liked the Tudor ghost, even if he did have a tendency toward matchmaking.

She walked along the hallway and heard footsteps behind her. Then a voice called out, "Lady Marjorie."

She turned and saw Miss Kent. The young woman offered a sympathetic smile and said, "I don't think we've met before, but I am Laurie Kent. I am friends with your sister Morgan."

And you were more than friends with Sir William, she thought to herself. But she decided to feign ignorance. "I am glad to meet you, Miss Kent."

"I saw you speaking with Sir William just now, and I thought we might talk a moment in private."

Because you want to warn me off, she thought. But there was truly no need for that, since Sir William was adamantly opposed to marriage. "Is something wrong?"

Miss Kent hesitated and stepped into the library. "You seemed quite taken with him, and I wondered if you were aware that he and I are engaged to marry." She spoke in the present tense, as if their past had disappeared.

"What do you mean?" Marjorie asked. She put on her best shocked expression as if she had never dreamed this would be the subject of their conversation. But inwardly, she was well aware that this woman felt threatened by her.

"My father forbade me to marry a man as poor as Sir William," Miss Kent continued. "They believed he was a fortune hunter, who would only take my dowry and use it for his own gain. I wept and pleaded, but Father insisted."

Marjorie resisted the urge to roll her eyes. She didn't believe that for a moment. If it were true, Miss Kent's father would have never agreed to the marriage in the first place, much less allowed their daughter to make plans. "Did you know he was poor?" she ventured.

Miss Kent sighed. "Not at first, no. But I heard from many of my friends that he had invested most of his family's fortune in spice shipments. My father warned me that he could lose everything."

Marjorie could not believe William had ever desired to marry such a fickle woman. "And you aren't worried about that now?"

She lifted her shoulders in a shrug. "Not anymore. I heard that he made a good profit from the investment, and he no longer has his fortune tied to the shipments." A moment later, Miss Kent shuddered. "My goodness, it's cold in here."

Marjorie could not see any of the castle ghosts, but she was silently cheering for them. "And now you wanted to warn me not to set my hopes on Sir William, am I right?"

"I should hate for you to have a broken heart," Miss Kent said quietly. "It would not be fair to you, when I have finally made my father realize that we love one another. Money is of no consequence anymore. William has all that he needs to take care of me."

The woman spoke as if she believed that. Even so, Marjorie wasn't about to argue, for she knew Sir William had no feelings at all toward herself.

"If you'll excuse me, I must go and see if my mother needs help." Marjorie nodded to Miss Kent and departed the library, not really knowing why the conversation had upset her. She and Sir William were friends, nothing more. Her feelings were a deep attraction, and she didn't want to marry anyone at all.

She passed by her sisters, Rose and Gwyn, but could not get close to Tamsyn or Morgan, due all the guests congratulating them. Instead, she decided to seek solace in the library, where she could gather her tangled up thoughts and put them to rights.

Quiet and solitude were her best allies now.

There were hours left until the Yule Ball, and she intended to spend them alone.

※

Later that evening, William searched for Lady Marjorie, but it seemed she had decided not to attend the Yule Ball. He couldn't understand why, for this was a celebration of her sisters' weddings. Of all people, she ought to be here.

To his annoyance, Laurie had practically stitched herself to his side. No matter where he turned, she was there. She wore a white gown embroidered with purple, and she laughed gaily during the celebration. Her mannerisms were filled with guile, and he doubted the sincerity of everything she said.

"Oh, William, I cannot tell you how glad I am to be at your side once more. I missed you *dreadfully*."

He thought of Marjorie's earlier comment, that Laurie had broken the engagement because of money. He wondered if that held any truth at all and decided to spin his own story.

"I was very angry when you left," he said quietly. "And over the past year, I thought of nothing else."

"As did I. I tormented myself with thoughts of what a mistake I made. We belong together,

William. We always have." She rested her hand in the crook of his arm, gazing at him in adoration.

He forced a smile he didn't feel. If she had truly believed that, she would have answered his letters. "I should tell you that I've made an important investment. One of my friends is going into copper mining, and I intend to help him." Only a few people knew about Michael Beck's plans, and he didn't want to mention it to anyone, especially in a lie.

Her face tightened with uncertainty. "What do you mean?"

"I think there could be a great deal of profit in copper mining. Unless of course, he chooses a site where there is no copper. It's a high risk, but I think one that will pay off."

"But...mining?" Her face fell at the thought. "You could lose everything."

"Oh, I doubt it," he said smoothly. "Besides, money means nothing to me. And of course, you have your dowry to support us, if needed."

Just as he'd suspected, she pulled her hand away. "I think that would be a grave mistake to invest, William. You mustn't think of taking such a risk." Her complexion had gone pale. "Do tell him that you've changed your mind."

"I've already given him most of my savings," he lied. "But I feel confident that—"

"You did what?" She stared at him in utter disbelief.

"You needn't worry," he reassured her. "If you truly believe we are meant to be together, it doesn't matter if we have money or not."

For a long moment, she was silent. The dismay on her face made it evident that Laurie was still deeply concerned about his wealth. He waited for the rise of anger, expecting to feel furious with her. Instead, curiously, he felt nothing at all, save impatience.

"Please forgive me, William, but there is someone I must speak with. I shall return in a moment, if you'll wait here." She gave a polite nod, and pasted on a smile as she crossed the room.

He could see the anxiety in her posture, and it struck him that her affection had dimmed the moment he'd suggested he might have risked his fortune on a mining venture. But more than that, he realized that he no longer cared about Laurie's approval. Instead, he found himself searching for a glimpse of Marjorie. He wanted to dance with her this night, to set aside the past and look toward a different future.

But she was nowhere to be found.

He moved through the crowd, grateful to be away from the throngs of people, until he was alone in the hallway. The noise of music and conversation filled up the space, and he walked past the garlands of greenery and colorful ribbons. This year, he had dreaded the thought of Christmas, for it had reminded him of Laurie. But now, he saw the greenery and remembered walking through the garden maze with Marjorie. He remembered the snowflakes falling upon her lashes and lips, and the honest smile upon her face.

In these past two days, he had come to enjoy that smile and her humor. Even when they were alone, with nothing but a Christmas pudding between them, she brought life to his battered heart. He didn't want to leave in the morning and never see her again. Instead, he found that he wanted her in a way he had never wanted Laurie, and the realization struck him hard.

Footsteps sounded behind him, and he turned to see Miss Cushing standing there. Her expression held disappointment, but she said quietly, "Marjorie is in the library."

William recognized her unspoken peace offering and said, "Thank you for telling me. And...I'm sorry that it would not have been a good match between us, Miss Cushing. You are a true lady."

"It's all right. I am entirely too boring for someone like you." She sighed and folded her gloved hands.

He didn't want her to denigrate herself. "I suspect there is more to you than most men realize. And one day, you'll find the gentleman you deserve—someone far better than me. I will do what I can to help you." He smiled at her, and she answered it with a tentative one of her own.

"Perhaps." She scrutinized him a moment and asked, "Are you planning to marry my cousin?"

He didn't know how to answer that, so he said, "That depends on her wishes. She doesn't seem eager to be married at all." But he could not deny that the idea of spending time each day with Marjorie was a welcome one.

Miss Cushing seemed lost in thought for a moment. "No, but she did seem to like you when I saw you together yesterday." With a twisted smile, she added, "Perhaps you'll want *me* to indulge in matchmaking."

"I would be grateful for your assistance," he answered honestly. If he could gain Marjorie's assent, he would speak with her father in the morning.

"I will think about it." She studied him a moment and then added, "I suppose I shall go join the wallflowers at the Yule ball."

"You deserve better than that," he said. "And if I might offer some advice, you should smile more, Miss Cushing. You look lovely when you do."

She did smile then, and curtsied to him before she returned to the ballroom.

William walked along the hallway toward the library, trying to assemble his thoughts. He didn't know why Marjorie had avoided the ball, but he hoped he had not offended her in some way.

As Miss Cushing had said, he found her curled up in a chair in the library, a book upon her lap. Beside her, a cup of tea rested on a table and it appeared to have gone cold.

"I thought you would be at the Yule ball," he said to her. "I wanted to dance with you."

Marjorie glanced up and shook her head. "I decided not to go."

William pulled a chair across from her and asked, "Why not?"

She closed the book and set it aside. "I suppose because I didn't want to see you dancing with Miss Kent…remembering how much you loved her."

Her words were lined with sadness, enough to give him hope. He leaned in closer and said, "I thought I loved her. But I don't think I truly knew the woman she was."

"She came back to you, though. And she reminded me that you are engaged once again."

William reached for her hands and shook his head. "We are not engaged."

Marjorie sat up, her eyes holding such emotions, he felt his own heartbeat quicken. "I told her a story of how I invested all my money in Beck's copper mine. She was appalled."

The faint smile at her lips gave him reason to hope. "And did you?"

He met her gaze squarely. "Would it matter to you if I did?"

She shook her head. "It wouldn't matter to me if you had not a penny to your name."

"I'm afraid I will have to disappoint you," he said, leaning in to brush his mouth against hers. "For I have a great many pennies that I would like to share with you."

She moved her hands to rest against his cravat. Her eyes held a sudden hope, and he threaded his hands in her hair. To his surprise, instead of holly, he found mistletoe tucked beneath the strands. He withdrew the sprig and held it out. "I don't think you need this here, Lady Marjorie."

Her face flushed, and she let out a slight laugh. "I blame Gwyn. I thought it was only holly in my hair."

He leaned in, nipping her lips with his. "I would thank your sister instead of blaming her. Because I think you need to be well kissed. Every day."

She wound her arms around his neck. "I agree."

This time, she brought her mouth to his, and he claimed it fully, drawing her onto his lap. He kissed her over and over, savoring her sweet mouth until her body trembled against his.

"Someone could walk in on us," he reminded her. "This is dangerous."

"Stay with me," she murmured. In her voice, he heard the longing, and it echoed his own feelings. He wanted this woman badly—more than he'd ever thought possible.

He lifted her into his arms and stood. "Where do you want to go? The kitchens? Or the maze?" He lowered her to stand before him, and she took his hand, leading him to the far side of the library.

Then she pressed at a panel beside one of the bookcases, and it clicked open. He could see nothing in the darkness, but she stepped into the hidden passage and drew him inside. A sudden rush of uneasiness passed over him, and his heartbeat quickened. Though he knew Marjorie only wanted a stolen moment, he didn't like closed spaces at all. For a moment, his heartbeat quickened, and it grew difficult to breathe. He wanted to get out of this place, but then Marjorie lifted her mouth to his, and he forgot about everything else. There was a faint sliver of light, enough to remind him that they could leave at any moment. She calmed him and with her in his arms, he was able to push past the discomfort.

He closed his eyes, shutting out all else except the feeling of her mouth upon his. She met his intensity with her own kiss, and when he slid his tongue into her mouth, she trembled. This time, he wanted to touch her, to make her feel the same wildness he did.

He drew his hands over her shoulders, lowering his mouth to the skin above her bodice. Her hands dug into his back, and she whispered, "I know this is wrong, Sir William. But I cannot stop the way I feel."

But he didn't want her to believe that any part of this was wrong. For he was falling in love with this woman.

"Will you let me touch you, Marjorie?" he asked quietly.

She was silent, and he drew his hands down her spine to the curve of her bottom. She gasped, and he kissed her again. With his mouth upon hers, he murmured, "If you want me to stop, say the word, and I will."

༄

Marjorie knew she should speak. She should tell him to stop, for this would only end in scandal. But she could not deny that she craved his touch. Her mouth was swollen from his kiss, and her breasts were aching against her gown. William removed his gloves and knelt down, his bare hands moving beneath her skirts. He touched her ankles, sliding his hands higher, to caress her calves. Her knees went weak, and she leaned back against the wall, trying to catch her breath.

"Are you all right?" he asked. His voice was heavy with desire, and she could scarcely breathe.

"Y-yes," she moaned.

"Then don't move." He kept his hand upon one leg, her skirts bunched above her knees. "I want to pleasure you, Marjorie. I want to watch you come apart in my arms."

She didn't understand what he meant by that, but he supported her with one arm around her waist. Her legs were slightly parted, and he moved his hand past her garters and cupped the warmth of her bare thigh. Between her legs, she grew damp, and she tried to gather what was left of her self-control.

If she let this go any further, it *would* end in marriage. There could be no other outcome. He was touching her intimately, and Heaven help her, she didn't want him to stop.

His palm moved to cup her wetness, and she cried out at the intense sensation. She drew her arms around his neck, unable to grasp any control at all.

"I want you, Marjorie," he whispered in the dark. "I want you naked in my bed. I want you every morning when I awaken. And I want to hold you when I fall asleep at night." His words took apart her senses, and when he caressed her intimately, she felt a strong aching of pleasure. It made her arch against him, and she gasped as he moved his thumb against her hooded flesh.

"William," she breathed. She wanted him desperately, and her body would not be denied. He was gently pressing against her, in a rhythmic motion that spiraled deep within her womb. Her nipples were taut against her bodice, and she pressed against him, feeling the rise of pleasure.

"If you were mine, I would claim you every day." He slid a finger inside her wetness, and she cried out. Slowly, he plunged in and out, stretching her until she was breathing in rhythm. He added a second finger, and she lifted her mouth to his, kissing him hard. His tongue matched the penetration of his fingers, and she could imagine what it would feel like to have him inside her body.

She craved the invasion, welcoming it, and he quickened his pace.

"My God, I want to be inside you," he said. "And I want you to take me deep, until I can feel your body embracing mine."

At his words, she thrust against him, and the sudden motion quaked within her until a fierce tremor caught her core. He moved his fingers again, never stopping until she reached the peak of her need. Marjorie gripped his shoulders, not knowing what was happening as she shattered apart in his arms. The pleasure came over her in waves, and she held on to him in the darkness, unable to stop herself from shuddering.

For a long time, she held him, as the aftershocks claimed her. He removed his hand from between her legs and helped her straighten her skirts.

"Are you all right?" he asked.

"I don't know." She ought to be deeply embarrassed by what they had done, but her body was too satisfied to care.

He stole another kiss. "I want to marry you, Marjorie." He leaned in, pressing his forehead to hers.

His declaration made her falter, for she didn't know what to say. After the liberties she had just allowed, certainly he would think she wanted to marry him. And yet, she hesitated, not quite knowing what it was she wanted. He had never spoken of love—only desire.

"I will speak to your father in the morning," he said. "With his consent, we can make the right arrangements."

She felt a sudden rise of confusion gathering within her. He was already assuming he had her consent—and she had not told him otherwise.

Before she could say a word, there were footsteps. The door to the passageway was pushed open, and she blinked at the brightness. Her father stood in front of her, and in the background, she saw her cousin Ariadne.

Lord Banfield glared at them both with fury, and Marjorie couldn't say a single word. Her own guilt was written upon her face.

"It looks as if there will be another marriage taking place," he said. His voice was like hardened iron, leaving no room for an argument.

"We will discuss it in the morning," Sir William said, stepping out of the passageway with her hand in his. "But yes, I do intend to wed Marjorie. I believe it would be best to have a small wedding, with only our immediate families attending."

"You will get a special license immediately," her father ordered.

She felt a numbness gathering hold of her as William and Lord Banfield began voicing plans for a wedding she hadn't actually agreed to. Once again, her life was being planned for her, and they were giving her no choice. She didn't want a marriage where she had no voice, where she was told what to do, where to go, and how to live her life.

"I am going to my room," she said quietly.

The two men hardly appeared to notice, but as she reached the door, William spoke up. "Lady Marjorie."

She turned and looked back at him, feeling overwhelmed by all of this.

"It will be all right," he reassured her. "I will handle everything. You have nothing to fear."

Nothing to fear except the loss of her freedom, she thought. At the moment, she could hardly gather any of her thoughts at all. She had been foolish enough to let her body's desires govern her common sense—and now, she regretted what she'd done.

From the stern look on his face, she doubted if her father would let her out of the marriage, even if that was what she wanted. A sense of panic doubled up inside her.

"I will see you in the morning and let you know what we have decided," he said.

Of course. They would make all the plans without her. And when it was all over, she would be trapped within marriage, unable to be herself at all.

Just like before.

Chapter Five

The next morning, William discussed wedding plans with Lord Banfield. He had never imagined he would find another woman whom he wanted to wed so soon. And yet, the thought of joining his life with Marjorie's was a welcome one. She was nothing at all like Laurie, and every moment he'd spent with her had been enjoyable.

"Where is she?" Lord Banfield demanded, when a footman brought them tea. "I told Marjorie to be here an hour ago."

The servant only shook his head. "We have not seen her, my lord. Lady Rose said she went out riding."

"It's Christmas morning," the earl muttered. "She has no reason to be out riding. I should have known she would try to avoid us."

Within a few moments, Lady Banfield joined them. The matron had a kindly face, and she sat across from her husband. "Merry Christmas, Sir William. I understand you have offered for Marjorie's hand."

"Merry Christmas," he bade her. "And yes, Lady Banfield. I would very much like to marry your daughter."

"Except that she's gone off on her own." The earl sighed. "Marjorie has always been a bit of a wild foal, doing whatever she pleased. I don't envy you trying to rein her in."

At that, Lady Banfield rolled her eyes. "I'm certain she will return soon, Allan. In the meantime, now that the pair of you have made your plans for the license, I should like to speak to Sir William about Marjorie's…previous fiancé, Viscount Dewbury."

William was taken aback by the countess's remark. Marjorie had said nothing about being engaged before. He waited for her to continue, and Lady Banfield folded her hands in her lap.

"I suppose you know that my Marjorie is rather reluctant to wed. And after her last suitor, I cannot blame her. Lord Dewbury was quite demanding."

His mood tightened as he wondered what she meant by that. Had Dewbury forced Marjorie in any way?

"Do I need to call him out?" he asked quietly.

Lady Banfield laughed lightly, as if he were joking. Which he wasn't. The thought of another man laying a hand upon Marjorie infuriated him. "No, she ended their engagement."

"Did he threaten her in any way?" He tried to keep his voice calm, but could not suppress the surge of dark jealousy.

The countess shook her head. "He was overbearing toward her. Nothing harmful, but he told her which parties they would attend and what she should wear."

"And what she could or could not eat," he predicted, remembering what Marjorie had said about having no freedom at all. The pieces fell into place, and he understood her reluctance to wed. She would not want any man to tell her what to do.

Lady Banfield paled, but nodded. "Why yes, that's right. I had no idea Lord Dewbury was attempting to manage her life in such a rigid way."

"He was only trying to take care of her," Banfield interrupted. "Some men want obedient wives."

The countess leveled him with a stare. "If you had dared to force me to leave a soiree, in order to change my gown because you did not approve, it would be the very last day we spent in each other's company, Allan."

"He was harmless," the earl argued.

"Marjorie didn't deserve him. And nothing she ever did was good enough to please him."

William sat in silence while the pair of them argued. It was beginning to make sense why Marjorie had been so upset about them being caught together. Both he and her father had started to make plans without asking her opinion. They had simply told her what to do and when the wedding would be.

It was little wonder that she'd fled.

A sudden fear slid over him, that she might not want to marry him. What if she wanted nothing to do with him and would rather run away than face a marriage?

Or worst of all, what if she turned her back on him and did not show up at the wedding, just as Laurie had abandoned him? He didn't want to think of that possibility at all. He cared about Marjorie... no, he loved her.

He wanted to spend his days with her, finding ways to make her smile. She deserved a marriage where her thoughts were valued, where he listened to her. And he intended to make that happen.

"Thank you for telling me about Lord Dewbury," he said to Lord and Lady Banfield. "I think we should wait on further wedding plans until I talk with Marjorie and see what *she* wants."

The countess's face softened. "I think that is a very good idea, Sir William."

He excused himself, realizing that he needed to find Marjorie and reassure her. This time, he would not make the mistake of telling her what to do. Instead, he wanted this marriage to be her choice.

It was Christmas morning, and it would indeed be difficult to make the arrangements he wanted. But he had several ideas on how to soften her affections and prove to her that he did care.

He nearly shook his head at his own idiocy. He had fallen in love with this woman and didn't want to spend a single day without her. If that meant courting her over the next few weeks until she agreed to marry him, he would do it.

For he didn't want this bride to run away.

༄

Marjorie gave her horse over to one of the grooms and was about to return to the house, when he said, "Lady Marjorie, Sir William asked if you would meet him in the gazebo."

She wanted to say no, for she didn't want to hear of all the wedding plans he and her father had arranged without her.

"Perhaps another time," she said.

But then the groom added, "He's been waiting for some time now, Lady Marjorie. Well over an hour. And I believe he has a gift for you."

She was reluctant to go, but decided that it would not be right to simply abandon William—especially since it was Christmas Day.

"All right." She started to walk toward the garden maze, when suddenly she heard the faint lilting sound of a lute. The music nearly made her smile. The Tudor ghost, Benedict, was meddling again.

When she reached the entrance of the maze, she was surprised to find a small plate with a single tea biscuit on it. What on earth was this? Was it William's attempt at a Christmas present?

Marjorie picked up the plate and took a few steps into the maze. A little further on, she saw a second plate with a piece of gingerbread upon it.

The third plate held sugared almonds, and at that, she began to smile. He was leaving a trail for her to follow, just as she had dropped holly berries during her last visit to the maze. By the time she reached the gazebo, she had a plate filled with all manner of sweets and desserts.

William was waiting for her, and beside him, she saw a plate of spice cake.

"Merry Christmas," he said, rising to his feet.

"This is a lot of food," she told William, setting the plate down on the floor of the gazebo. "I never expected you to lure me into the maze with so many desserts."

He reached out for her hands, and she went to stand before him. His blue eyes studied her with such yearning, her heart beat faster. "I needed to apologize to you, Marjorie. I hope you'll hear me out."

She didn't know quite what to say, but waited for him to continue.

"I never meant to force you into marriage," he said quietly. "It is, and always has been, your choice whether you want to marry me or not."

The sincerity in his voice was reassuring, and she was glad that he was no longer behaving like Lord Dewbury. It seemed as if the invisible chains were breaking apart, and she relaxed in his presence.

"I never imagined I would want to marry again," he said. "Especially after Laurie left me. But you are like no woman I've ever known. I find that I want to be with you, whether we are playing cards, eating gingerbread, or dueling with forks."

The aching of emotion rose up within her, and she felt her eyes filling up with tears. "I want to be with you, too, William."

His hands squeezed hers. "But I was wrong to make plans without you. I spoke in haste because I didn't want to lose you—not because I was trying to take away your choices." He reached out for the plate of cake. "You said once before that you would marry cake if you could. I am asking if you will marry me instead. And I promise you may enjoy cake every day, if that's what you want."

Her heart lightened at his words, and she broke off a piece of the cake. Instead of eating it, she placed it in his mouth. "Only if I can share it with you, William."

He set the cake down and took her in his arms, kissing her hard. "I'm in love with you, Marjorie Hambly. Will you marry me?"

She tasted the hint of cinnamon upon his lips and wound her arms around his neck. "I will. Because I love you, too."

Outside, a few flakes of snow began to drift all around them, and she heard the sweet melody of Benedict's song. William drew her into his arms, warming her in his embrace. From his pocket, he pulled out a sprig of mistletoe that he'd taken from the Great Hall.

"I brought this, for I thought it might be needed." He held it over them, leaning in to kiss the woman he wanted to share his life with.

Marjorie only laughed and took the mistletoe, tossing it aside. "You're wrong. We don't need it at all." Then she pulled him down into a deep kiss, reminding him of how much he loved this woman.

And William Crandall decided that Christmas was the best holiday of all.

※

If you enjoyed "The Sweetest Christmas"
and would like to try another story for FREE,
sign up for my author newsletter here:
http://www.michellewillingham.com/contact/

You'll receive a download link to the story after
you confirm your subscription. I only send out
newsletters when I have new releases or when
there's an amazing book sale, and you may
unsubscribe at any time.

Did you miss the first story in the Castle Keyvnor series, featuring Marjorie's friend Jane? Keep reading for an excerpt of

A DANCE WITH THE DEVIL

Chapter One

Autumn, 1811

"They say Castle Keyvnor is haunted."

"Don't be silly. There's no such thing as ghosts." Jane Hawkins considered herself to be a sensible young woman. She didn't believe in anything of the supernatural variety, and she rather thought the spirits of the dead had better things to do than frighten the living. Her friend, Lady Marjorie, was of another mind and appeared deliciously scared at the idea.

"I've heard that late at night, sometimes you can hear the ghost of Lady Banfield wailing for her lost son," Marjorie murmured. "What if we see her in the hallway?" She shuddered at the thought. "I cannot imagine anything worse."

"We're going to be fine. I imagine people exaggerate the story because it makes it more interesting." Despite her attempt to reassure Marjorie, Jane couldn't help but admit to herself that the castle was not exactly the sort described in fairy stories—no, this was a castle that would terrify small children. Tall and imposing, formed from dark stone, Castle Keyvnor stood upon the edge of the sea cliff with turrets rising against the shadows. The darkening evening skies added to its somber presence.

"At least *you* don't have to live here," Marjorie muttered. "I, on the other hand, am doomed. Unless I can find a gentleman to marry who will take me away from this horrible place." She glanced over at her mother and sister, who were sleeping on opposite sides of the coach. "Why did my father have to acquire a castle like this?"

Lady Marjorie's father, Allan Hambly, had inherited the earldom of Banfield, which meant he would reside at Castle Keyvnor for some time. Several other families had traveled for the reading of the late Earl of Banfield's will, and Marjorie had insisted that Jane come with them.

Her stomach twisted in knots at the thought. She didn't belong here with all the nobility. She was a vicar's daughter, and though she and Marjorie had been friends since they were young girls, Jane knew her place.

"We're going to find a husband for you, too," Marjorie insisted. Her friend smiled brightly, but Jane didn't share her optimism. Yes, a husband would indeed help her circumstances. Her parents were aging, and Jane doubted if there was enough money to support them for very much longer. She had to either marry or find a position as a governess or a companion.

No one wants to marry a vicar's daughter, she reminded herself. She had no dowry to speak of and no title. Marjorie meant well, but Jane knew the reality of her situation. At best, she might wed a merchant or a soldier. But her chances of marrying well were not good.

"I think you have a better chance of finding a husband," she told Marjorie. "I'm no one. At least you're an earl's daughter."

"Don't denigrate yourself," her friend insisted. "You're quite beautiful. And if there's a wealthy titled gentleman, I'm certain he'll be besotted with you."

Jane didn't argue, though she was a realist by nature. There would be no offers from titled lords—not for someone like her. She understood that, even if Marjorie didn't.

The coach slowed as it traveled down the narrow lane leading toward the coast. A light rain spattered against the window of their coach, and Jane pulled her shawl closer in anticipation of the cold. "I'll be glad to stop traveling," she told her friend. The wheels had jolted them over every rock and rut in the road until it felt as if her teeth were rattling out of her skull.

"So will I. Though I imagine my knees will still be shaking." Marjorie grimaced as she glanced back at her mother and older sister Tamsyn, once again. "I don't know how they're sleeping through this." Her other three sisters had traveled in a second coach with their father. Jane was grateful not to be crammed inside with them, or worse, having to ride with the servants.

A few minutes later, the coach came to a stop, and a footman opened the door to the coach. At that, Lady Banfield awakened, along with Tamsyn.

"Heavens, what a terrible journey," Lady Banfield moaned. "I will be glad to sleep in a bed of my own this night."

"So will I." Tamsyn yawned and stretched. She accepted help from the footman as she disembarked from the coach, followed by her mother and sister. Jane waited to be the last one out of the vehicle, being careful to keep a slight distance from the family.

It was startling to see so many other coaches also arriving at Castle Keyvnor. Jane counted at least four others, and all around her, servants were busy unloading baggage.

"You'd best stay with the family, Miss Hawkins," the footman warned. "With so many people about, it's safer."

She nodded and trailed behind Marjorie and her mother. The afternoon light was waning as evening approached. When Jane took another step closer to them, a violent gust of wind caught at her shawl. She tried to seize the wet wool, but the gust tore it from her fingers and sent it flying toward a group of guests.

"Oh dear," she murmured, hurrying after it. It was the only shawl she owned, and in cold weather such as this, she could not afford to lose the garment.

To her horror, she saw it tumble upon the ground, the wind tossing it until it came to rest at a gentleman's feet. He was busy speaking with another man, and Jane didn't dare approach.

He might move away. If he did, then she could snatch it quickly, and no one need know. But already she could see the Banfield family walking toward the drawbridge over the dry moat. She ought to be with them, but instead, she was chasing after her errant shawl.

The gentleman's expression transformed a moment, and then he bent down, picking up the sodden, gray wool. "What have we here?"

"It looks as if that maid has lost her shawl," the other man teased.

I'm not a maid, she wanted to tell them, but didn't. She didn't truly belong here and had only come at Marjorie's insistence.

But when the first gentleman turned to face her, Jane felt her face grow red. Goodness. This man was surely an angel, fallen from Heaven. Or perhaps a devil. His blond hair was tipped with darker ends, and his green eyes were like Connemara marble. He had a strong jaw that hinted of wickedness, and his mouth was firm and held the hint of a smile. He was exactly the sort of gentleman who might steal a lady into dark corners. And worse, she would enjoy it.

"Have you lost something?" the man asked, holding out the shawl.

Jane nodded, unable to speak. The English language had fled her mouth, and if she'd tried to speak a single word, surely she would have failed.

After a moment, while the man continued to offer the shawl, she realized that she was supposed to actually reach out and take it. Good Lord, she had clearly lost her brain.

"Th—thank you," she stammered as she accepted the shawl. "My lord."

With a nod to him, she fled back toward Marjorie and the others, hurrying until she reached the drawbridge. Her cheeks were burning with embarrassment. And yet, she wondered if the man was as attractive as she'd imagined.

She knew she shouldn't look back, but could not resist the urge. The moment she turned, she saw him staring at her. Not with unkindness or with a harmful intent…but almost as if he found her to be a curiosity. Jane pulled the wet shawl across her shoulders, tightening it as if it were a shield.

And then he smiled at her, tipping his hat.

ତ

"She's not for you."

Devon Lancaster, fourth son of Viscount Newbury, glanced over at his best friend, Jack Hazelwood, Lord St. Giles. "And why not? She's beautiful."

The young lady who had lost her shawl had a heart-shaped face, framed by light brown hair and blue eyes the color of cornflowers. She was painfully shy, but Devon found himself intrigued by her.

"Because she's a servant, that's why." Jack dismissed her immediately. "She might be fair enough for a tête–à–tête, but she's not meant for marriage."

"Why would you assume that?" He hadn't seen the young lady carrying any baggage for Lord Banfield or his family. It seemed that she had hurried to catch up to one of the earl's daughters.

"Because of her clothing. Now if you're looking for a rich wife, you should look toward Banfield's daughters or Beck's relations. Anyone except Lady Cassandra, that is. Otherwise, I'll gut you." Jack offered a friendly smile, but Devon knew better than to even look toward Lady Cassandra Priske. His best friend had invited himself to Castle Keyvnor for the sole purpose of courting the lady—not because he expected to inherit anything from the late earl. He had arrived the day before, along with their mutual friends, Michael Beck, Teddy Lockwood, and Hal Mort.

As for himself, Devon had come along with his own purpose, which also had nothing to do with the will-reading—he wanted to find a wife. And though he knew what was expected of him—to woo a wealthy, respectable woman—he wouldn't mind finding someone who captivated him.

"I wouldn't dream of even looking in Lady

Cassandra's direction," Devon said. "But I must admit, finding a wife is a daunting proposition. Marriage is so very...permanent." His own parents had an arranged union that was civil, but neither of them had felt any sort of affection toward one another. If anything, his mother had held a great deal of animosity toward the viscount, due to his numerous affairs.

Devon didn't want that sort of marriage. Perhaps it was a ridiculous idea, but he preferred to have affection toward his wife. He wanted someone who was a friend as well as the future mother of his children. That, at least, would make the marriage bearable. And if she happened to be beautiful with a passionate nature, he wouldn't mind that, either.

He joined Jack as they walked back toward the drawbridge. It was early evening, but the sun had not yet descended. "Has Lady Cassandra arrived?"

His friend shrugged. "Not yet, that I know of."

They crossed over the drawbridge, beneath an ancient iron portcullis. The moment he crossed into the outer bailey, Devon felt as if something icy had brushed his shoulder. He glanced at his friend, who didn't appear to notice anything. Then, the chilly sensation vanished, leaving him to wonder if he'd imagined it.

Still, he couldn't help but broach the idea. "What

do you know about Castle Keyvnor?" asked. "Do you think it's true that the place has ghosts?"

"I doubt it. But Beck did point out a spot where they apparently beheaded a man." Jack pointed toward a patch of green lawn within the courtyard. "They said he was a traitor to King Henry VIII." His expression darkened. "Beck thinks this castle is cursed. I simply think it's old. Everything creaks when it's seven hundred years old."

Devon hung back a moment, motioning for Jack to do the same. The young woman whose shawl he'd rescued was standing a few paces behind the Earl of Banfield. He studied her more closely and realized that Jack was right. Her clothing was very plain—she wore a dark blue serge gown and the gray shawl he'd rescued earlier, along with a gray bonnet. Her light brown hair was bound up away from her face, and her blue eyes were downcast.

But in spite of her plain attire, he couldn't quite tear his gaze from her. There was something about her face that drew him in, making him wonder about her secrets.

What would she look like with her hair down around her shoulders, those blue eyes staring back at him with interest? Her body was thin, but there was no denying the curve of her breasts or the gentle sway of her hips.

Devon wanted to know her name—needed to know it. No, she likely wasn't a candidate for marriage. But there was no harm in getting acquainted with the lady and finding out why she was here.

"Beck invited me to play a game of billiards," Jack told him. "Do you want to come?"

Devon shook his head. "I've another challenge in mind." With a nod toward the young lady, he added, "I'll wish you luck in your game."

"One doesn't need luck when one possesses great skill. You are welcome to join us in a later game, if you enjoy losing."

"I might," Devon agreed.

Just then, he heard the sound of barking. A small black poodle raced toward the center of the courtyard, snarling at the empty air. The hair on the dog's spine stood on end, and he growled at the unseen enemy. It was the very spot where Jack claimed the traitor's beheading had taken place.

"Are you certain the dog hasn't seen a ghost?" Devon teased. Though he had never actually witnessed a specter, he hadn't imagined the icy chill that had passed over him.

"I doubt it. But dogs do sense things." At that, the animal lifted his leg and proceeded to relieve himself upon the execution site.

Devon bit back a grin. "Well, if there was a ghost there, I imagine he is quite put out."

"Or marked." Jack shook his head and started toward the castle keep. "In the meantime, I'll bid you good hunting with your mysterious servant girl."

"She's not a servant. Her speech is too refined for that." Her tone and diction were nothing at all like a servant's. And yet, he hadn't missed the way the woman held herself back from Lord Banfield's family. She appeared too young to be a governess, truthfully.

But he intended to find out exactly who she was.

Jane had never felt so overwhelmed in all her life. Castle Keyvnor was the largest estate she had ever seen. After enjoying a cup of tea and a light repast, she had walked behind Lord Banfield and his daughters, staring in bewilderment at all the rooms. The stone walls and Gothic architecture reminded her of a medieval castle, especially with the large tapestries upon the walls.

"I'll need a map," she said to Marjorie. "I'm going to get lost in this place."

"So will I," her friend agreed. "But as long as we get lost with a handsome gentleman to guide us back, it's all right by me." Marjorie leaned in closer. "Did you ever find out the name of the man who gave back your shawl?"

Jane blinked a moment. "I didn't realize you saw that."

"I notice *everything*." Marjorie smiled at her. "And once I find out who it is, I will ask Father to introduce you."

"Don't bother. If he possesses a title, he will have no interest in a vicar's daughter." She gripped the edges of her gray shawl, well aware of her plain appearance. Every garment she owned was gray, dark blue, or brown, and modest, as befit a clergyman's daughter.

"He might," her friend offered, though Jane didn't believe it. All of a sudden, a barking noise caught her attention, and she spied a black poodle racing down the hallway.

"Oscar! Come back!" a young woman called out, hurrying toward the dog. Jane saw the animal bolt around the corner and on impulse, she decided to help.

"I'll be back," she said, as she picked up her skirts and hurried after the dog. She had three dogs of her own at home and had no doubt she could help retrieve the animal.

"You'll get lost!" Marjorie warned.

"Then I will ask for directions and find you again." Jane smiled and raced around the corner, just in time to see the poodle change directions again. He skidded to a halt in front of a stone staircase, and she slowed her pace. If she ran toward him, he would consider it a game and scamper away once again. Instead, she took slow footsteps.

"You're a mischievous fellow," she remarked to the dog. "Why did you run away?" The dog wagged its tail at her, and she suspected he was only playing.

"Do you need help, my lady?" came a male voice from behind her.

Jane turned and saw the very gentleman who had rescued her shawl. Oh dear. Of all the men to find her, why did it have to be the man who tied her tongue into knots?

"I—yes, I think so. He got away from one of the ladies, and I thought I would try to retrieve him." She tried to keep her attention squarely upon the poodle, for if she dared to look at the gentleman, she would undoubtedly lose every coherent thought.

"That's kind of you." He drew closer and added, "I suppose I should introduce myself, since there is no one here to do it properly. I am Devon Lancaster."

For a second, she'd thought he'd said Devil

Lancaster. He did indeed resemble a devilish sort of man, with his dark blond hair and green eyes.

"And you are Lord of what?" she blurted out without thinking. Heavens, what was wrong with her? She wanted to knock her head against the wall. "I'm sorry. I meant only that—that is, your title—"

"I don't have one," he answered cheerfully. "I'm the fourth son of Viscount Newbury. I'm nothing but a mister." He eyed the dog and took another step toward him. "And you are?"

"Jane Hawkins," she answered. "Also Lady of nothing. I'm a friend of Lady Marjorie's."

"Any relation to the late earl?" he asked.

"None at all." She offered a sheepish smile. "I feel like an imposter, just for being here. Marjorie insisted that I come with her family, but I don't really belong."

Mr. Lancaster leaned in and murmured, "Don't tell anyone, but I shouldn't be here either. I'm friends with Lord St. Giles and Lord Michael Beck, and I joined them at their invitation."

"Then we're both imposters." Jane relaxed somewhat, for it did feel that neither one of them ought to be here. And now that she knew he was not a titled lord, she felt less conspicuous.

"So we are." He took another step toward the dog, who was sniffing at the steps and snarling.

"I'm going to pick him up on the count of three. I think I can come up behind him before he notices. One…"

"I don't think he's going to let you do that." Her own dogs would delight in racing away, provoking her to chase after them.

"Two." Mr. Lancaster held up his hand in a pause. "Three." He lunged toward the poodle, who shot across the hallway in a full run.

"Blast it." He took off after the dog, and Jane joined him in a run, laughing as she did.

"I told you he wouldn't let you seize him." She gripped her skirts while her shawl slipped down her shoulders. "Dogs love to be chased. Or at least, mine do."

"What do you suggest?"

They continued running down another narrow hallway until the dog scampered halfway to the end.

"We need to corner him," Jane said, huffing as she kept up with Mr. Lancaster. "If we can trap him inside one of the rooms, that will do. And then we can find his owner."

"Good idea." He motioned for her to spread out, and they slowed their pace as they reached the end of the hallway.

"Oscar!" The young woman who owned the dog

came running toward them, her dark hair falling loose from its chignon.

"Don't worry, we'll help you catch him," Mr. Lancaster reassured the woman. "Let's try to drive him toward an open room, and we can close the door."

"How about the room at the end of that hallway," Jane suggested. "You could run ahead of the dog and cut him off so he can't go down the other way."

"All right. And the two of you try to herd him inside." Mr. Lancaster moved toward the end of the hallway, racing past Oscar to block his path. As he took a step toward the animal, the poodle scampered in the opposite direction—exactly as they'd hoped.

"Perfect," Jane said. "Now let's guide him toward the doorway." She joined with the other young woman, and as they moved forward, Jane introduced herself and Mr. Lancaster.

"I am Lady Cassandra Priske," the woman answered. "Thank you so much for helping me catch up to Oscar."

"You're welcome." Jane offered a friendly smile, and when Oscar saw the pair of them approaching, he ran into the room. "Trapped," she proclaimed in triumph.

"Bless you both." Lady Cassandra hurried after him, and Jane blocked the doorway so the poodle ould not run away. She thought about joining Lady Cassandra, but stopped herself when she realized there were two gentlemen already inside the billiards room.

"I think she has control of her dog once more," Mr. Lancaster said. "You did well, Miss Hawkins."

She stepped away from the billiards room, feeling her cheeks warm beneath his praise. "So did you. And now I am hopelessly lost within this castle. I don't suppose you know the way back to the drawing room?"

"I do indeed. Will you allow me to escort you there?" He offered his arm. "And if we find any escaped animals along the way, I am certain we will manage well enough."

His charming smile slipped past her defenses, making her all too aware of his masculinity. She rested her hand upon the crook of his arm, feeling her heartbeat stammer within her chest.

This isn't real, she reminded herself. *He's only being a gentleman.*

And yet, she was entirely too conscious of the way his coat clung to his broad shoulders. His green eyes gleamed with a blend of amusement and a hint of wickedness.

When they reached the drawing room, Jane felt the need to apologize. "I am sorry to have disturbed you," she said. "I imagine you never intended to spend your evening chasing after a poodle."

"No," he agreed. "But were it not for Oscar's misbehavior, I might not have met you, Miss Hawkins. And it was a pleasure, indeed."

Chapter Two

"It was a mistake to bring her with us," Regina Hambly, Lady Banfield, said to her husband. She motioned for the elderly footman to bring the tea tray, and the servant obeyed, setting it down on the end table. Regina poured two cups, adding a nip of sugar to her husband's tea.

"We had no choice," the earl countered. "She was summoned."

"But it will only cause a scandal if anyone finds out who Jane really is. If they discover that she's—"

"They won't." The earl took his cup and sat across from her. "I see no reason to tell her anything. Let Jane believe she is here as Marjorie's companion. And if we are careful, we can arrange to give her whatever portion she is entitled to, without anyone ever learning the truth."

Regina steepled her fingers together and nodded

toward the footman. "Bronson, leave us, if you will."

The older servant had difficulty hearing and likely hadn't heard a word of their conversation, but she didn't want to take any chances. Once he had closed the door behind him, she turned back to Allan. "We have no idea how much Jonathan Hambly left her. If it's a small amount, no one will think anything of it, and we can hide the scandal. But if he left her a fortune, everyone will want to know why."

"We will handle that once we know." Lord Banfield straightened. "For now, we will keep her identity quiet. I think it would be best."

"Sometimes I wish we had sent her away." Regina sighed. When Jane was born, they had felt sorry for the newborn child. A child born out of wedlock could never have a respectable life. It had seemed kinder to let her be raised by the vicar and his wife instead of sending her to an orphanage. At least Jane had been given a home with a loving family. Regina had thought it a perfect solution at the time, never imagining that the past would come back to threaten everything.

"We did the right thing for Jane," Allan said quietly. "I believe that."

She moved beside him and took his hand. "I am

only glad that Evelyn did not live to hear about Jane. It would have broken her spirit."

Her husband squeezed her palm. "No one can know of this, Regina. Especially Jane."

"It will be our secret."

෴

"You should come with us to breakfast, Jane," Marjorie said. "Why would you take a tray in your room? Don't you want to see Mr. Lancaster again?"

Jane mustered a smile and shook her head. "It's better if I stay here. I really don't belong with everyone else."

Marjorie frowned. "And what about me? And Tamsyn and Rose and Morgan and Gwyn? You don't think you're worthy of eating with *us*?" Her friend rolled her eyes.

"That's different. I've known you all my life." Marjorie was practically a sister to her, as were the other girls. They had played together as children and not once had the girls looked down on her, despite their family's comfortable wealth.

But her true reason for avoiding public gatherings was a sense that she didn't truly belong among the nobility. Everyone else had been summoned to receive a portion of their inheritance. Jane was merely here as a companion.

Marjorie sighed. "Jane, you must come. Otherwise, you're behaving like a long-suffering martyr."

The invisible blow was more hurtful than she'd imagined. Jane tightened her lips and admitted, "All of my clothing was handed down to me. Whenever I'm around the other ladies, I cannot help but feel their disapproval."

"Then borrow one of my gowns."

"I cannot do that, Marjorie. It would be a lie. This is who I am. I'm not trying to behave like an heiress."

Her friend rolled her eyes and opened her trunk. She rummaged around until she found a white long-sleeved muslin gown. It was very plain with only a bit of ribbon trim along the hem and cuffs. "Wear this. And if you do not, I will have Tamsyn hold you down while I dress you. You are coming with us to breakfast, or we will drag you by your hair."

Her pride burned at the thought. "There's no need for this, Marjorie."

"Good. Then you must realize that my sisters drive me into madness. I need you there as my friend so I won't murder them. You're keeping me from being arrested."

Marjorie waved her maid to come over. "Penny, help Jane into this gown." She crossed her arms and waited.

Although Jane felt like a caterpillar being pinned with butterfly wings, she held still and allowed Penny to dress her in a chemise and short stays. The gown had no buttons and the maid helped slide it over her head, pulling the laces tightly around the bodice to fit it to her. Jane sent a dismayed look toward Marjorie. "I look as if one good sneeze would cause me to pop out of this."

Her friend smiled brightly. "Well, that *would* give us an interesting discussion over breakfast, wouldn't it? Do try to keep your bosom under wraps."

Jane seized a pillow and swatted her friend while Marjorie giggled. "Careful, or you might tear a seam."

A knock came at the door, and she heard the voice of Lady Tamsyn calling out, "Are you both ready?"

"Not yet. But come in and see Jane," Marjorie answered.

Her older sister opened the door, and the moment Tamsyn spied Jane, she smiled. "You do look beautiful."

The white gown made her feel entirely too conspicuous. "I still don't think this is a good idea. It doesn't truly fit, and I—"

"Nonsense," Marjorie took her hand and half-dragged her to the door. "You're coming with us, and that is final."

Lady Tamsyn took her other hand. "I couldn't agree more."

Despite her misgivings, Jane promised herself that she would try not to speak very much and blend in as well as she could. One meal might not be so bad.

But her stomach was twisted into knots of vicious nerves. In this gown, every curve was accentuated, and she worried that the other guests would get the wrong idea about her. They might believe she was one of the ladies meant to inherit.

She followed Marjorie and Tamsyn into the dining room and saw several other guests milling about. The room reminded her of a cathedral with its tall Gothic windows and the ribbed vaulted ceiling. Upon the wall, she saw four pointed stone arches, and a fire burned in the hearth behind the large mahogany table.

Lord and Lady Banfield greeted their daughters and nodded a welcome to Jane. She steeled herself and followed Marjorie to the sideboard where she took a plate. A short older man with graying hair stood behind her. He smiled brightly, "Good morning to you. I don't believe we've met as of yet.

I am John Hunt, solicitor to the late Earl of Banfield."

Jane nodded in greeting. "Good morning." With an apologetic shrug, she said, "I'm not related to Lord Banfield. I am Jane Hawkins, a friend of Lady Marjorie's. I came as her companion." She chose a slice of toast for her plate, along with a spoonful of strawberry jam.

The solicitor blinked a moment. "Didn't Lord Banfield tell you? You were summoned along with the others. In fact, it was *most* important that you be here, Miss Hawkins."

"Let's not speak of this right now," Lord Banfield interrupted. With a sharp look toward Mr. Hunt, he stood beside Jane. "She is here, and that is all that matters." The solicitor muttered an apology and took a step back.

But Jane felt as if the floor had dropped out from beneath her. "What is Mr. Hunt talking about, Lord Banfield?"

"We will discuss this in private," the earl promised. "Not in front of all these people." Again, he glared at the solicitor. "Is that quite clear, Mr. Hunt?"

The solicitor seemed taken aback. "Do you mean to say that she doesn't know?"

"Know what?" A sense of alarm had gathered

inside her. Mr. Hunt was behaving as if she were related to the late earl.

But the new Lord Banfield stepped between them. In a low voice, he added, "One more word from you, Mr. Hunt, and I will deduct a portion of your salary."

"Well." The solicitor let out a sigh of air and added, "Don't the eggs look delicious? I believe I shall have to try some."

But Jane had lost her appetite. Her mind was reeling from the solicitor's revelation. To Marjorie, she whispered, "What was your father talking about?"

Her friend appeared just as bewildered. "I have no idea." She took Jane by the hand and brought her to the table. Leaning in, she added, "But I promise you, I will find out everything." She beamed and whispered, "Wouldn't it be wonderful if you turned out to be a secret heiress?"

Jane picked at her toast, swirling the strawberry jam in a circle around the surface. "I don't know about that."

She had always known she was adopted. The vicar and his wife had made certain she was aware of her birth circumstances. Her real mother, Emily Hawkins, had been a governess in the household of a neighboring family, before she had been seduced and left pregnant. Once she had begun to show, she had been dismissed at once from her post.

The Hambly family had felt sorry for Emily's plight and had arranged for her to stay with the vicar and his wife, John and Mary Engelmeyer. The Engelmeyers had taken Emily into their home, offering to raise the baby as their own. But the young woman had died in childbirth, and it was a miracle that Jane had survived.

We were so grateful that the good Lord blessed us with you, her adopted mother, Mary had told her. *I could not have children of my own, but I thank God every day that your mother gave you into our care.*

Jane had never known any other parents, save the Engelmeyers, but it hadn't mattered. They had loved her and reared her as their own. Now, it felt as if her safe life had been ripped apart. Her real father was somehow related to the Earl of Banfield, it seemed.

What if he was here now, at Castle Keyvnor? Her mind couldn't quite grasp it, and she pushed her plate away, untouched.

"Are you all right, Jane?" Marjorie asked.

"I think I need to take a walk. Some fresh air might help," she admitted. She stood from her chair and pulled her gray shawl over her shoulders.

Just as she was leaving the dining room, she nearly bumped into Mr. Lancaster. He wore a bottle green coat and buff-colored breeches. His expression turned warm, and he teased, "Are you fleeing at the sight of me, Miss Hawkins?"

Her cheeks flushed. "No, I simply thought I'd take a walk after breakfast."

"It looks as if it will rain," he pointed out. She bit her lip, feeling foolish for not even considering the weather. And when she glanced at the dining room window, she realized he was right. Dark clouds hovered in the sky and a light sprinkling of rain was spattering against the glass, sliding down in rivulets.

"Well, then, I suppose I shall simply explore the house."

"Be wary of the ghosts," he warned, with a light smile. "Beck was telling me about a screaming noise he heard from one of the turrets. Or it could have been the wind."

"I don't believe in ghosts," she said. "But thank you for the warning." She couldn't help but smile in return, and her heart fluttered at the intense warmth in his green eyes. He was staring at her with unconcealed interest.

"You look lovely this morning. The gown suits you." His deep voice warmed her, and Jane felt her blush deepen at his compliment. She wasn't accustomed to men noticing her, and she hardly knew how to respond. She almost blurted out, *It's Marjorie's,* but thought better of it and simply voiced a thank you.

"Enjoy your breakfast," she bade him. "I'll go wandering through the halls instead of outside."

Mr. Lancaster's smile faded, and he turned serious. "You'd better take an escort with you. While I don't think anyone here would harm a lady, it's never wise to go anywhere alone."

She gave a noncommittal nod. "I understand." Though truthfully, she didn't really want to be around anyone just now. Her friends were all enjoying their breakfasts, and she'd lost all appetite for food after Mr. Hunt's revelation. Right now, she wanted a moment to be alone and think about what to do.

Lord Banfield held the answers she wanted. It was clear that he'd known she was meant to be here. But why? No one had ever told her anything about her father, except that he had seduced her mother and left her. A tightness gathered in her stomach. She didn't want to meet the man, even if he *was* here. Anyone who would take advantage of a woman and then leave her behind with a pregnancy deserved absolutely nothing.

She excused herself, but before she could go, Marjorie handed her a note. "Jane, I was asked to give you this."

She took the message and opened it. Lady Banfield asked to meet with her in the kitchen in private. Jane wasn't certain why she had chosen that location, but the countess might be busy planning the menu for tonight's dinner with the cook. It was a strange note, but she saw no reason to question it.

Perhaps Lady Banfield would have the answers Jane was searching for.

Would you like to read more?
"A Dance with the Devil" is available in print from Amazon or the author's website here:
www.michellewillingham.com/book/a-dance-with-the-devil/

It can also be downloaded from all e-book retailers.

Kindle bestselling author and Rita® Award finalist **Michelle Willingham** has published more than forty romance novels and novellas. Currently, she lives in Virginia with her children, and is working on more historical romance books in a variety of settings, such as medieval and Viking-era Ireland, medieval Scotland, and Victorian and Regency England. When she's not writing, Michelle enjoys baking, playing the piano, and avoiding exercise at all costs. Her books have been translated into languages around the world and are also available in audio. Visit her website to find English and foreign translations.

www.michellewillingham.com

Made in the USA
Coppell, TX
19 July 2025

52106324R00090